War & Music

A Medley of Love

MAX EVANS

UNIVERSITY OF NEW MEXICO PRESS
Albuquerque

Library of Congress Cataloging-in-Publication Data

Evans, Max, 1924–
War and music : a medley of love / by Max Evans.
    p. cm.
ISBN 978-0-8263-4908-8 (alk. paper)
1. World War, 1939–1945—France—Fiction.
2. Soldiers—Fiction.
3. Music—Psychological aspects—Fiction.
4. Normandy (France)—Fiction.
I. Title.

PS3555.V23W37 2010
813'.54—dc22
                        2009051957

A Dedication from the Heart

To the VA Hospital of Albuquerque and their sterling team of doctors, nurses, staff, and volunteers who, along with my wife, Pat, kept me together enough to finally finish my last novel, *War and Music: A Medley of Love.*

To the Dr. Roland Sanchez family for their deep friendship and the years of successful work we shared on the Farm and Ranch Heritage Museum of Las Cruces, New Mexico.

To decades-long friend Luther Wilson, the best fly fisherman I have ever known. He made this sport both an art and a science. With fond remembrances of the fine entertaining and most productive years we shared at gone-forever Baca's restaurant.

To "brother" Billy Marchiondo, who is the most special of things to me; an unequivocally loyal friend.

To our twin daughters, Charlotte and Sheryl, with love, who have—often with great struggle—shared a lifetime of extreme ups and downs in the uncertain world of the arts, but are successful nonetheless.

To the special villages of Ropes (Ropesville), and Andrews, Texas, Des Moines, Humble City, Taos, and Hillsboro, New Mexico, with all our friends therein in whatever dimension they currently inhabit.

one

He didn't know who he was, and he had no idea where he was on this earth. He struggled to focus. He saw a grain field but the blurry images were only a kaleidoscope of colors. He couldn't think. He was dizzy and sick. He stumbled along until he fell into the soft dirt. Straining upward to his hands and knees, he began to heave until his ribs groaned and only a trickle of moisture was left hanging from his lips. He wanted to sink to the soil and into the roots and become part of the crop.

He sat up and tried to see where he was. The cloudy roundness began to form edges and shapes that held briefly. With a mighty effort he willed his body upright. There right before him was a bench—if it would just stop moving back and forth. He forced himself to remain stationary until he could become truly aware of something—anything. At last, just before he fell again, he managed to get hold of the back of the bench and propel himself around it so he could sit down. There was an echoing in his ears becoming stronger, clearer.

The sounds of war are known by those who have participated in infantry combat. The screaming preparatory anguish of artillery shells. Their different calibrated explosions of destruction are instantly recognizable. The shallow coughs of mortars as they arc their shells into the air unheard until a final whisper just before the whacking explosion of disaster. Then there is the snap of broken air as the fire of machine guns and rifles breaks the sound barrier above one's head. There are the different, distinctive sounds of rockets, hand grenades, rifle grenades, and even pistols if the fighting is at close range. In the background are the intermingled sounds of fighter planes diving and strafing and the delayed heavy thump of bombs, along with all the iron-clanking death machines—the tanks and their weapons, the supply trucks and other mechanized war instruments. It is a serenade of devastation for the amusement of chuckling demons. A symphony. Then . . . then, "Oh, my God! God help me!" "Mama." "Mama." "Medic, medic, medic." "Oh, God, please." That's how the joke of sorts got started: "There are no atheists in foxholes."

The ripping of flesh, the cracking of the bone it hangs onto, the seeping or spurting of blood make sounds that certain insects and worms relish hearing. And the loudest sound amid the medleys of war is that rarest of moments when all is quiet, impossibly quiet.

The soldier, who now sat on the bench in the middle of a grain field, heard the silence that was cracked into pieces by the cawing of a distant crow and those who answered the "caw, caw, caw." He blinked without being aware of it, still trying to see where he was. Finally he opened his eyes wide and held the view for a long moment.

He could see the heavily vine-covered hedgerows angling on three sides. Farther on there were different-shaped clumps of trees. The sky was a soft almost milky blue with little strings of clouds so thin their edges were transparent. He took a deep breath, and the smell was what made clarity of mind begin to begin.

The beast of war belches and passes almost endless odors. There is the acrid smell of freshly detonated gunpowder and burnt steel. There is the sweet scent of newly freed blood misting above the dead, dying, and mutilated bodies, little red streams forming pools that begin to turn brownish as they seep slowly into the bruised earth. There is a special combined smell when a shell penetrates, explodes, and sets fire to a tank—a mixture of steel, powder, human flesh, bone, and blood, gasoline and oil, clothing, and stained and torn family photos.

Then there is the unforgettable stench of bodies long past the first discovery of the flies. This is a forever odor. So is the scent of villages, towns, and cities burning.

As the Infantry Corporal started to go back, he touched his head and realized there was no helmet on it. He rubbed the dirt out of his short hair and felt for his rifle. It was absent as well, but the .45 automatic was in its holster. He recognized a familiar smell. It was some farmer's precious milk cow. The feel of the gun and the smell of the cow, which seemed to be coming from beneath him, created action. He stood up, the unsteadiness gone. Suddenly he realized that the bench he had been sitting on was a hugely swollen cow with its four legs sticking up, and slightly out, in a silent stretch. One was shorter than the other three. A foot had been blown away.

He turned slowly around, making a complete circle. There were no soldiers, no jeeps, no trucks, tanks, or artillery pieces, no movement that would take away a single life. It was eerily peaceful.

The jagged shreds of his memory circled and collided. Sounds and scents mingled in a vortex of war. He could only think of climbing out of the confusion and maybe running round and round the world until it all vanished. His ears popped, and he could hear his own living breath again. Then he was looking into the deep blue eyes of his best friend, Sergeant Emilio Cortez, and remembering the last lost hours.

Corporal Ty Hale had gone to school, trained, partied, and now fought beside Emilio. They had become instant friends because they were both from New Mexico, although they had been raised a couple hundred miles apart. Ty was born to stock farmer parents on the great flat plains a few miles north of Lovington in Lea County in the far southeastern part of the state. Sergeant Emilio Cortez came from Las Vegas, New Mexico, in San Miguel County on the edge of the north central mountains.

Ty Hale had lost his parents and older sister in a flash flood on a trip to visit the nearby Carlsbad Caverns. He had been taken in by his grandparents. They owned one of the few irrigated farms in the area, only a few miles from his birth home. The local people were desperately working to survive the Great Depression and dust bowl. The discovery of oil fields south of Hobbs gave the area a boost. The desperate need for fuel for the war with Germany and Japan helped, but recovery was agonizingly slow.

Ty hunted rabbits, dove, and quail to help at his grandparents' table. He loved the vastness, even the amazing flatness on a round world to hunt in and became a "dead shot" with his .22 Winchester pump action rifle.

His grandparents were Martha and Jiggs Hale, but Ty had his own names for them from as soon as he could talk: Mama Jo and Papa J. They were hardworking, proud people. Even in the worst of times their place looked well-kept and prosperous. There were no loose fence wires or boards, nor piles of manure from the livestock—that was hauled to a compost pile and spread yearly on the fields for fertilizer. Everything was always in proper order. Jiggs insisted on all stock farm endeavors being taken care of, as he called it, "first cabin." That meant all the tools were cleaned before they were put in the spot they were supposed to be—and the next time Jiggs Hale needed to use one it better be there. He was a weather-seasoned, well educated old stock farmer who worked Ty hard but treated him kindly when he did his work with sweat and truth.

His grandmother spoiled him in some ways. She read to him a lot and frequently surprised him with certain favorite dishes, and she taught him the wash-hands-face-and-behind-the-ears habits of personal cleanliness. She washed, ironed, and hung his clothes like a grand opera singer's personal assistant. Since Ty had always called her Mama Jo, gradually all the neighbors picked up on it and it became her name for good. In secret she was very proud of it.

Jiggs loved playing his old Victrola in the early evening and often asked Ty to sit with him and listen. The music wasn't always what Ty was exactly interested in, but he listened to please his grandfather. Ty tried not to fidget. He watched his grandmother in her rocking chair embroidering, crocheting, or something like that and just wished he had something to do to keep from thinking about all the great fun things he could be doing outside at this very moment. Accidentally one evening he found out that reading was allowed while listening to great music. His grandparents had read to him regularly and insisted that Ty read some of the classics. Jack London was his favorite. They also saw to it that Ty perused *Life* magazine and *Popular Mechanics*.

At first, Ty resented this intrusion on his free time, but soon the books and magazines, like the fields and the prairies, became a natural and enjoyable part of his life—just like Jiggs had said they would.

Jiggs, with his sharp, dark eyes smiling from a weather-seared face, used to say, "I tell you what, son, if a man is really lucky he'll find that what he wants to do is what he likes to do. That is, of course, if he's lucky enough to take the time to discover it."

Whenever Jiggs spoke, Ty turned his own dark eyes, set in a pleasing face, straight at Jiggs and really heard what his grandfather said, even if he disagreed.

Jiggs didn't drink around the house out of respect for Martha. Her father had been a born-again drunk, so she forbade the use of liquor in her clean house. Jiggs respected this and hid a bottle or so in the barn. When Jiggs went to town to shop for supplies he usually took Ty with him, but sometimes, when he wanted to go alone, he gave Ty some chores to do and said simply, "I got the town-thirsties."

In the middle of a grain field in Normandy when he couldn't, even with great effort, straighten out a single thought, Corporal Hale allowed Papa J to slip into his mind. He felt for his canteen. It was there and was almost full. God, he was thirsty as a sandstorm. He drank half the contents without stopping, and then his training took over and he saved the rest to ration.

Why was he thinking of his grandfather Jiggs when the blue eyes of his best friend kept pulsating back and forth from life to death in the space before his own eyes?

two

For two days Jiggs had been curing his "thirsties." Before facing Martha, he dropped by the corral that Ty was repairing. He stood so still and so quiet it could be heard all over Lea County. "Son," he said, "you'll find only a few people who can or will deliver the goods. Treasure them. You hear?"

Ty thought to himself, "*I don't know what that has to do with me repairing this corral.*" But he answered, "I hear you, Papa J. I hear."

Jiggs's voice faded, and Ty caught only the last of a story, ". . . he knocked ole Joe in the head with a full bottle of whisky—broke it all to hell and wasted it." And Jiggs turned and went to face Martha.

In a grain field in Normandy, a confused Corporal Hale suddenly remembered something of home. He remembered how he had always loved to run. If he was hunting afoot and it was over for the day, he would run all the way home. It paid off unexpectedly when he became a track star at Lovington High, and then it earned him a scholarship to Highlands University, a small college in Las Vegas, New Mexico, where he would have his first, fateful meeting with blue-eyed Emilio, who had received a similar scholarship. Emilio used his height to high jump for the track team.

As beginning buddies do, Ty had casually mentioned that he'd overheard his grandfather saying to his grandmother, "That Ty is always running for the far horizon, but it keeps moving ahead of him," and Martha had answered as always in his favor, "Yes, he is. And someday he'll catch it, and it'll be downhill from then on."

Emilio saw the humor in this semi-seriousness and came right back with one from his own father. "Papa says the most lasting laughter should be at our silly, ridiculous selves."

Together they had chuckled at the wisdom of their elders. The same sense of humor makes instant friends, and they would be friends as long as they both had breath. And they would honor those elders by remembering their sayings, thereby enjoying themselves at the same time.

Soon Ty seemed to be a part of Emilio's family and grew to feel at home with the kind of food one can only find in northern New Mexico. Emilio's mother seemed to take pride in Ty's always favorable comments about her cooking, especially her use of green chile.

Emilio's older brother worked for the forest service in Colorado. His father, olive-skinned and gray-eyed with a fine straight nose over a whitened mustache, was a retired railroader who had many old friends to visit around town and a few to go fishing with him in the nearby mountain streams.

Emilio's eighteen-year-old sister, Elena, was responsive to everything in life from sports to the outdoors to her family. She had the same blue eyes as Emilio, with a lithe but full figure, and her hair was as black as moonless midnight, with a bluish sheen in certain lights. Ty could hardly keep his eyes from following her every fluid movement. But somehow, he did, feeling instinctively that he would be infringing on his friendship with Emilio and on the Cortez family's welcome. Nevertheless the thought of trying to date her nagged at him constantly. She would soon be graduating from high school and intended to attend the University of New Mexico in Albuquerque and major in journalism. Ty thought she should head straight for New York.

When Ty was in Lea County, he had loved hunting on the great prairies that had been mighty cattle ranches before drought and depression had taken most of the cattle. He had believed at the time that this was the way the world had always been and would always be. But here in Las Vegas he could look across a million acres of foothills beyond the rolling prairie. They undulated on up and up into northern New Mexico's part of the Rockies, where white-iced peaks reflected air so pure it attracted artists from all over the world.

Several times, Emilio had taken Ty to the mountains to fish for trout. Every trip was special and different. The gurgling, forever-twisting little snowmelts coursing, playing, singing over millions of differently shaped stones deeply fascinated a young man from the dry, flat plains of Lea County. It was a gift of beauty sparkling in the sunlight to out glimmer all the diamonds in the world. He believed it. He would have wagered on it. Emilio had introduced him to a ceaseless wonder. A brand new world—and the fishing was almost as exciting. He could never stop marveling that these small streams could be home to foot-long brown and rainbow trout.

Fascinated as he was by the mule deer, coyotes, the birds of the forest and the timbered hills and mountains, they were no more beautiful to Ty than the lonely prairies. They were just different. The prairie sky was far bigger than the earth and sometimes there was nothing but a flat horizon to look at. He loved them equally and felt completely blessed. Ty had two families and lived in two worlds that he loved, one on the prairies and one in the mountains. He had the best of all. How many people were so privileged?

One day after classes, Emilio said, "There's something I've been wanting to show you, Ty."

They walked and walked through the old western streets of Las Vegas and entered a cemetery. Ty followed as a determined

Emilio went straight to a large, well-tended grave site. He stopped wordlessly and stared. Ty saw that the elegant stones were carved with the Star of David beside the cross, but were inscribed with a Spanish surname.

After crossing himself Emilio said, "Those are my great-great-grandparents. Many of their blood followed them here. They had much to do with the growth and welfare of this town. This whole area of New Mexico, for that matter."

Ty was silent. It would seem sacrilegious to say anything.

They walked back towards the entrance. Emilio pointed at the small Star of David near a central cross. After a moment he spoke. "My great-aunt was really something special, they tell me."

There was no more wondering about the blue eyes of Emilio and Elena.

As they walked towards the plaza, Emilio explained, "Long ago, oh, in the late 1400s or early 1500s, the Jews in Spain and Portugal were forced to convert to the Catholic faith during the Portuguese and Spanish Inquisition."

Ty asked, "What if they didn't wish to change?"

"Well, they would be crucified, so the decision to change was pretty basic, regardless of what their hearts and faith told them."

"Survival is a very strong decision maker."

"Yeah, and not only did they convert but they adopted Spanish names to ease the suppression. In secrecy, mostly, they were called Conversos—the converted." Emilio continued his history lesson. "A lot of them followed the Conquistadors to the northern part of Mexico and then on into what was to be New Mexico and southern Colorado. We all know about this in a vague way. Many around here still secretly practice Jewish traditions. Traditions like: all wild life when killed is hung head down, throat slit to drain all blood as the Jewish faith demands. Little things are still prevalent."

"Will it ever be admitted or accepted, do you think?" Ty asked.

"Oh, there's more research beginning. So more light, in certain areas, will slowly shine on the Conversos and the Spanish as brothers and sisters."

"It's hard to accept that this sort of stigma exists in the U.S."

"Yeah, I know, but when you really think about it, there's all kinds around the whole world I suppose. And worse prejudices, at that."

It seemed to Ty that Emilio must be a cousin or a friend of everyone in Las Vegas. So many people stopped to talk to him and ask about his family, he was having a hard time showing Ty all the Jewish businesses in the downtown area. Emilio pointed out a huge warehouse owned and run by the Ilfeld family. They sold and delivered a wide variety of wholesale goods throughout the entire state.

"Those folks came to New Mexico from many lands. I'll take you soon to another cemetery, one where a Star of David and Jewish surnames are on almost all the headstones. They were a powerful force in New Mexico's development, and we still appreciate them."

They walked silently for several blocks. Finally Emilio said "I'm swearing you to secrecy, amigo, and I feel guilty for telling you, but here goes. There is a secret room in our basement where both mom and dad go to worship in Jewish. They even light the menorah there during Hanukkah."

Ty made a zipping motion over his mouth and said, "It stays here, amigo." He looked up at a bar sign they were passing and said, "Hey, let's go in here and have a beer, Emilio. Okay?"

"Sure. My cousin runs the place."

There was so much natural beauty around this quiet New Mexico spot. The sparkling snow-born streams, the unique architecture, and the clear, strong light that drew painters from the world over. But even this beautiful little town couldn't escape the War Beast. They all sensed the coming tide of blood. The red/gray imaging of battle-murder was immersed in all their minds. It was in their nature if not their fate. Everyone was affected. People heard about Hitler on the radio. There was more talk of war now than about the Friday night basketball game or politics or even religion, the town's main sport for scores of years. Worry about the war was becoming dominant. Almost everyone agreed that it would be better to fight across the waters than in their own land, blessed with such beauty.

Pearl Harbor was the greatest of all mistakes for the Japanese. The attack went straight to the ancient war genes festering in American souls. Day by day those genes, mostly dormant for the last twenty-five years, were headed for the brain, swelling and irritating mightily. The only known cure was action and reaction. It had always been so. Patriotism ran high.

Ty and Emilio signed up for the Army after being sworn to by the recruiter that they would serve together in the same regiment no matter what. Ty went back to big, flat, lonesome Lea County, to say goodbye.

His grandmother stuffed him with all his favorite foods, and his grandfather took him quail hunting.

Jiggs said, "Since I was in the last big one, I know personally there are things one Infantryman should hear from another. Don't ever fear crying out to the Great Mystery in the Sky. History is loaded with great minds who have totally failed to explain a particle about gravity, or for that matter the mystery of incomparable music composed by Beethoven even after he went stone-deaf." He looked Ty straight in the eye. "For centuries great mathematicians and other geniuses have been puzzled by Time and Change. They remain among the great imponderables. Heck, even the finest meteorologists' weather predictions cannot be deemed accurate unless they have already happened. Do you understand me?"

"Yes, I do, Papa J." And he prayed that he did.

Ty left his birth land to return briefly to his second home, Las Vegas, New Mexico, where he would, he must, join his best friend Emilio Cortez for the beginning of their long journey together. Maybe endless. He also had to give his possible last respects to Emilio's parents and the just-growing-up young sister, Elena.

While waiting for their appointment with the Army recruiters to receive their assignment, Emilo and Ty decided to take one last fishing trip to Taos. Without saying so, both knew they might never have another chance.

Elena unexpectedly volunteered her company (with her parents' permission) on this venture. The boys were both surprised and pleased, for she was very good company and excelled at camp cooking—though if truth be told, there was nothing Elena did that Ty didn't wholeheartedly appreciate.

They packed their sleeping bags and fishing gear in the trunk of the old Ford sedan. Elena and her mother had prepared homemade tortillas, eggs, canned meat, cheese, and assorted goodies and chunks of ice for the insulated box. They were all set.

Elena insisted that she ride in the backseat to—as she put it–"watch after the food and contemplate her navel." Although said with a wry smile, this remark put many other thoughts in young Ty's mind.

They took the dirt road to Mora and wound up the steep, twisting road of Holman Hill to the tiny village of Chacon. At this point they could go to the right and arrive in Taos about twenty-five miles later, or take the longer way through Peñasco and Dixon, where the rough, curving graveled road turned into a paved highway. They took a vote. It was unanimous. The longer way won.

They decided to take a tiny detour to check out the Rio Grande before they headed north. Its swift, green water was something they wanted to remember while they were away at war. They decided not to stop here to fish. Today they all preferred the small mountain creeks.

After the long hill at Pilar they topped out to one of the great views of the world. Over a million acres of earth greeted their eyes where the Rio Grande Gorge split the earth hundreds of feet deep. Sprinkled with blue-green sagebrush and cedar, the desert rose slowly on the west from the mighty gorge. The sky was massive, and the constantly changing cloud formations were as dramatic as a Shakespearean murder or a final love scene. Every day, every hour, Taos has many skies.

To the north of Taos village looms the magic Taos Mountain, forest-covered except where mighty bluffs bulge out like a champion boxer's chest. This mountain is proud and powerfully welcoming at the same time, talking and singing in a different voice to everyone with the soul to listen. Below the mountain sits the multistoried Taos Pueblo, long the tallest edifice in New Mexico. The village of Taos spreads nearby on the valley floor. Six different flags have been unfurled on its plaza. It looks as if it had been lifted out of the earth by a giant force and patted here and there by a mighty hand to shape homes and store buildings from the dirt. Almost every structure was made of adobe and plastered with smooth mud.

The three were silent in awe until Elena whispered, "Oh, my God!"

They circled Taos plaza before heading for Twining Creek. They had been here many times before but the scenes never grew stale. The Indians in Arab-like blankets were leaning on a rail next to the plaza visiting and watching the people watching them. Some saddle horses were tied to the wooden rails. Three or four wagons and their horse teams waited patiently for their masters in a vacant lot adjoining the plaza. Scattered cars with the license plates of several states, mostly Texas, were parked all around the plaza, their previous occupants wandering about window-shopping in fascination at the exquisite silver and turquoise jewelry, Navajo rugs, paintings and Indian pottery. With some reluctance the trio headed out of town toward Hondo Canyon and Twining Creek. The magical mountain seemed to dominate not only Taos Valley now, but the entire world.

As Emilio drove, Ty looked to his right across some irrigated pastures and small farms at the pueblo. Ever since he had first seen it and visited it, he had been captivated. He had read everything he could on its history since the arrival of white people; before that the pueblo's history was purely oral, and he had no way of hearing any of that. In the last few hundred years the people of the pueblo had survived events beyond imagining. There were constant attacks from the Apaches and even the Plains Comanches upon their person and their granaries. Then came the Spanish invaders, followed by the mountain men trapping from their watering places, then the miners prospecting these same streams and mountains. Even the battle to kick the Spaniards all the way back to Mexico had started here. Finally the Taos Pueblo had to accept the gringo occupation. The last of the invasions was the tourists and artists who settled there from around the world. In Ty's mind the people of the Taos Pueblo were simply the greatest survivors on earth.

When the trio left the tiny villages of Arroyo Seco and Hondo they entered the steep timber-covered canyon of Twining Creek, all three minds came back to the world around them. The cool mountain air seemed to be created by a superior spirit to lull them into a deep feeling of peace.

They made camp, pitching a tent on a rise above the creek in case of a sudden mountain shower. The creek came from 12,800 feet on Bull of the Woods Mountain. The mountain was out of sight, hidden by its bulging lower flanks, but the stream rippled and gleamed like liquid jewels as the late afternoon sun managed to beam shafts of light among the aspen, spruce, and pines as it moved towards the hidden horizon.

The boys gathered firewood as Elena insisted on building the fire herself. Emilio got his fly rod out and to everyone's surprise caught three rainbows from ten to twelve inches long in time for supper. Ty dressed out the fish and Elena fried them over an open fire. They feasted, then kept the fire going a while after dark, but their usual small talk of school, of future, of fun things petered out earlier than usual. The tent was small, and Ty made sure Emilio's bedroll was between his and Elena's.

A soft mountain breeze drifted down the canyon and tossed the tree limbs in uneven rhythm. The creek had its own rippling ceaseless sounds. Way off an owl hooted and an unknown night bird sounded and was answered from far away. Unknown insects hummed their personal tunes. The music of the canyon night enhanced the sound sleep of youth.

The next morning when Ty and Emilio dressed and crawled from the tent they barely had time to wash their faces and hands before Elena yelled, "Come and get it or I'll throw it to the fishes." She had managed bacon, hot tortillas and an open jar of her mother's salsa to put on the scrambled eggs. They ate ravenously as the sun moved above the canyon walls and warmed the earth and the three youngsters. She insisted on cleaning and putting everything away saying. "You guys go fishing," she said. "All the fish may be gone from Europe by the time you get there. Just remember, we have to leave this paradise by noon. So get fishing."

Ty walked along the creek, but back a ways so as not to jar the earth when he found a fishing hole that looked and felt right. He eased up and dropped the two hooks softly into the blue hole that differed from the now sparkling emerald stream. He had baited two hooks, one with a worm, the other with salmon eggs. He waited, staring into the water, willing the fish to feed. He waited. Then the tug came strong and solid. He jerked the hook out of the water so hard he threw the fish back, causing it to jar free from the hook. It flopped about falling down the slope towards the creek. He dropped his pole and dived for the slippery fish. A fat ten-incher. He was breathing from excitement as if he had finished a fast lap around a one-mile track. He slipped the chain through the fish's gills, letting it slip into the cold water to stay fresh. He caught an eight-incher next. Ordinarily he would have thrown it back, but not today. Time was limited, and he wanted one more fish fry with the parents of his companions who had treated him as one of their own for three years now.

Soon he had moved at least half a mile down creek and had seven fish on his string. He was almost ready to quit as the sun was getting near the noon position when he felt the heaviest tug so far. Again he over-jerked, and the one-footer was tossed into the bushes behind him. As he turned to get up, he looked straight into a pair of eyes as blue as a Mayan worship pond. They picked up little emerald flashes from Twining creek. He was suddenly numb. Elena had squatted there in silence watching him. Such a moment comes so rarely that one can only make an instant decision, one that may change your life. Right or wrong, he reluctantly sought the twelve-inch trout, trying to think only of her parents' enjoyment in eating it.

"Ah, Ty, that is a beautiful catch," she said, rising to her feet. Her jeans, tight and perfect below her blue shirt, enhancing the eyes that Ty was now trying to avoid. Why? He couldn't coordinate his thoughts enough to come up with an answer. Whatever—it was was done. In such moments entire lives are decided.

They walked side by side back to the campsite. Elena had already packed everything. She had an inner compulsion to give all she could to the two young men soon to depart their beloved land for the faraway unknown. Emilio soon arrived from upstream. He had caught his limit of an even dozen. At least, at the very least, there would be one last fish fry in Las Vegas, New Mexico, San Miguel County, U.S.A.

As Emilio drove up out of the canyon past the village of Arroyo Seco they all became silent. Ty looked around Emilio at the mighty bulge in the earth above the valley and understood that he and his best friend might never see it again. The noonday sun blessed the very top of Taos Mountain.

Emilio drove towards Las Vegas. Ty's mind wandered and enveloped the vast grazing lands to the northeast of Las Vegas all the way into southeastern Colorado and the Panhandle of Oklahoma. Grass waved on millions of acres enriched by the volcanic dust of millions of years back. Cattle, horses, antelope, deer, bobcats, coyotes, and crows dominated the mighty spread of land. Blue mesas snaked across the far horizons like giant snakes petrified in a timeless land.

Then there were the humans, scattered more than the animals. The ranch headquarters were mostly invisible. In the vastness the towns such as Clayton, Springer, Cimarron, Roy, and Raton were mere specks until the town limits were visible.

"Oh, God," he thought, "How will I do without this vision? How will I take these lost horizons with me?"

He didn't know it, but this very moment he was missing it more than he ever would again. Other lives, deaths, and lands would soon dominate his vision—maybe forever.

three

Now here in a Normandy field, surrounded by the fortress-like hedgerows, Corporal Ty Hale puzzled in an agony of bewilderment. He couldn't remember when or what had sent Emilio and him on the hour-and-a-half drive to Santa Fe to enlist. They had done so with the caveat that they would stay together. They were lied to, and yet miraculously after basic training they were assigned to the same division and eventually to the same squad. They had trained in Ireland and in the Welch mountains for the day of days in mechanized history, June 6, 1944.

They were in the infantry. They had loaded into LSTs twice, and twice climbed back up the criss-crossed rope ladders onto the ships. When gusts moved the curtains of smoke apart, they could see the tiny men both alive and dead—many dead—on the huge beach. The sounds from the allied ships firing in unison was so loud it killed thought, not to mention the soldiers it destroyed atop and below the bluff. The Navy had risked it all by moving in close to the shore with the rocks and jagged German steel pylons just below and all around them. They hung tough and blasted the enemy gun emplacements to bits. It turned the direction of the world.

On June the 7, when the LSTs finally took them to that hellacious and heroic beach, the ocean didn't care. It drowned the faint, the overloaded, and the plain unlucky, but most made it onto the sand amid only intermittent artillery fire. Before they made the climb in an indentation in the bluff they could see around a thousand slicker-covered bodies still awaiting removal.

After reorganizing on French soil, they attacked, intending to take a German stronghold at Trévières. The fighting was bloody and extra difficult because the Germans had artillery zeroed in on critical spots. The German snipers had plenty of U.S. soldiers to fill their sights, and it was a machine gunner's delight as the U.S. infantry tried to advance across open fields between the hedgerows. The infantrymen were fighting without their heavy weapons. The shortage of engineers from the losses on June 6 had slowed the heavy weapons' delivery from the barges. But they took Trévières with the help of air force strafers and bombs.

The sights, smells, and sounds of war had become familiar to the survivors. Bloody, torn bodies, pale, still, and expressionless, soon became a norm amid the chaos. All the sounds of enemy mortars, automatic weapons, and the zoom zip boom of the 88s became as familiar as the clucking of a farmer's chickens. Knowing the sounds of death was how one lived. Men in the squad of Corporal Ty Hale and Sergeant Emilio Cortez had fallen, bled, and died. They were left behind for the medics at first and then for the meat wagons that picked up the dead. Losing the trusted friends of months and years was, at first, almost unbearable. But the men had to go on fighting forward no matter the immense feeling of loss. Something familiar and comforting gone, gone, gone. It was almost as hard to watch the surviving civilians looking into ruins of their ancient homes, destroyed by bombs and artillery, seeking something familiar of the past or the remains of a loved one: part of a prized object, a cross, a teapot, a leg, a hand, any bloody organ, a soul. Somehow, this stayed in Corporal Hale's mind longer than the dead buddies. They were mostly old men and women with the little children whose fathers had long gone to fight or join the resistance or to die.

About June 11 the Allied lines started fighting for a massive 1500-mile line. The Germans fought just as hard, but by July 20 the great uneven line was formed in a wiggly arc.

Replacements for the deceased and shattered living were filling the vacant ranks. The survivors of the Normandy invasion started singing to the scared new replacements a chorus of "You'll be sorry. You'll be sorry." It was a dirge that worked. At first the replacements felt a shiver of fear, and then slowly realized they had to accept this undeniable truth.

The hedgerow where Ty and his warrior companions were dug in varied from five to six feet tall. When moving back and forth with food, water, or orders, everyone ducked to avoid the occasional enemy rifle and machine gun fire from the next hedgerow and beyond.

Corporal Hale of Lovington, New Mexico, and his best friend in the world, Sergeant Emilio Cortez of Las Vegas, New Mexico, had dug and shoveled foxholes a few feet apart. The guns had been quiet for perhaps half an hour. They sat up on the edge of their earthen homes and talked of great fishing trips they would soon be on in the Sangre de Cristo Mountains and the girls they would choose and love forever. Their comforting conversation began to be interrupted now and then by a rifle bullet striking the hedgerow just above Emilio's head, where there was a smooth, almost barren crawlway for wild animals and infantry soldiers.

The enemy rifleman kept firing along the top of the hedgerow near them. Emilio was agitated that a single sniper was disturbing their brief moment of relief. It was as if someone was throwing rocks at your home, timed just far enough apart to keep you on edge. A moment now of peace. A fleeting precious time to share dreams before the devastation reached a new crescendo. A few moments was all they asked.

Just as Ty was regretting not moving on his friend's sister, Elena, thinking of her supple figure and imagining her wide blue eyes looking lovingly into his—it happened.

The German sniper fired again. The bullet ricocheted off into space, and Emilio leaped up with his rifle. Ty followed suit, shoving his rifle above some grass and vines that laced the rock hedgerow into a fortress. He was sighting at the distant German location when some slight sound pulled him to look at his friend. Emilio spun sideways and the two faced one another directly. The German bullet had just nicked the front center edge of Emilio's helmet and there was a little black hole just above the bridge of his nose. The great blue eyes, as blue as a Taos artist's sky, stared into the brown ones of Corporal Ty Hale, and their all-seeing liquidity turned to the dull opacity of unpolished marble. His being had vanished from him before his muscles had gone limp. He fell. He lay on one hip with his lower body twisted one way and the top of his torso another. One arm was trapped under him, the other outstretched as if reaching for something that had vanished before he could touch it.

Ty screamed, "Medic! Medic! Get the medics!" The cry was as wasted as a single snowflake on a ski run in summer. The brave medics came and straightened Emilio out and covered him with his slicker and carried him away on a stretcher. He was gone. There were hundreds of thousands nearby, all somehow connected, but Ty was alone—the only person left in all the world.

four

Orders to attack came down early the next day. The officers just above the battalion commanders had been ordered to straighten their lines as much as possible to prepare for the greatest bombing in all history just before the critical attempt to break through at Saint-Lô. They were only about twenty miles from the invasion beaches at this moment hanging on by their bloody fingernails.

Ty took charge of his and Emilio's squad, and as soon as the prelude of American artillery, dive bombers, and mortars had turned the air to dust, smoke, and some droplets of blood, he led the men down the outer wall of a hedge, falling in a watering ditch now and then, to escape small arms fire. Some didn't escape. A machine gun, dug in where the hedgerows just ahead criss-crossed one another, was holding everyone alive to a full stop. If they lifted their heads an inch above the little ditch at the wrong instant, oblivion would ensue. Corporal Hale, without a conscious thought, had unhooked a hand grenade. He made an instant leap up and forward pulling the grenade pin. As he saw the barrel of the machine gun turn his way, he hurled the grenade up, up, and out. He hit the ground face down as the grenade exploded. When he looked up to check out the results, he saw that floating dust now covered the dug-in machine gun.

He gathered his surviving men. The two wounded had to be assisted back to medical help. The dead were left where they lay.

The only care they needed could be supplied by the meat wagons or the worms.

As they neared the German emplacement with their rifles ready, bodies tense, hearts thumping unheard, unfelt, they saw a form hanging out of the gun emplacement. It was a blond-headed kid. He couldn't have been over twelve or thirteen. The grenade had blown his guts out the same as if he was thirty. Ty almost threw up.

Several U.S. units had passed the child soldier safely by hugging the outer edge of another hedgerow, but he had fired viciously at everything he could see until the grenade numbed his trigger finger. To the surprise of Ty and his men the body gave one last convulsion spitting a combination of bloody phlegm, blood and hate into Ty's face. He almost casually wiped it away with his sleeve as the small body went limp and the one visible blue eye became void.

Even with all the battle adrenaline pumping, Ty paused a moment staring almost blindly and spoke to his squad, to himself, to an unhearing world, "He was just a kid." Then repeated very softly, "Just a little kid."

They moved on down the hedgerow, preparing to dig in. The enemy had retreated and had dug in only one hedgerow beyond. Now a huge war of attrition began. The long lines of facing men were more or less static, but patrols from both sides collided and fought. The bleeding and dying never stopped.

The Germans controlled Hill 192 fronting the town of Saint-Lô. They looked down the throats of the Americans for miles directing artillery their way. Most of the fire hit roadways and supply routes, slowing troop movements. The Germans dug and punched holes under the hedgerows, and a single hidden and well-protected machine gun could stop an entire battalion's advance. They set mines and trip wires as well as cross-firing weapons.

A great American weakness in the early hedgerow war was their tanks. When a tank rolled up to cross a hedgerow, its lightly armored underbelly was exposed and the tank became a death trap. At last a plain-old-country-boy sergeant figured out that by taking German steel traps from the beach, cutting them to a short length and welding them in a pointed V shape to the front of American tanks, they could burst right straight through. It worked.

In the purposeful stalemate the U.S. infantry trained to follow the tanks through the corridors ripped in the hedgerows. Of course, there was still Hill 192 to take before a true breakout at Saint-Lô could be achieved. If this could be done, then the armored divisions could come into play as the hedgerows thinned farther on. Ah, plans. Plans of great battles to come on the blood-drinking earth.

But there was another plan. The Allied Forces would strike from the air the morning of July 10 and pulverize the enemy. First, the American artillery would fire smoke shells just ahead of their lines to show the planes their targets. It was the greatest plan ever conceived. Except it didn't exactly work.

No one in any of the hundreds of thousands of foxholes slept much that night. Ty Hale didn't even doze. How could he? They would know just after the daylight launch if the greatest ever combined-air-and-land military attack had worked.

They first heard it as a low hum that was reassuring, even soft, like a fine orchestra just beginning to play. Then louder but still a hum, and now the heavens were rent as never before by humans. The birds of death were black against the violet sky, countless shapes and formations all part of one massive arc as far in both directions as even the dimmest-eyed soldier could see.

One, two, three, a dozen, a hundred, thousands of groundlings sat on the edges of their foxholes, their tanks and artillery pieces. The drivers of jeeps, tanks, and trucks were awestruck at the seemingly endless thousands of planes and their combined sounds rending the sky as they drew closer to annihilate the enemy. There had never been anything like it, nor could there ever be again. With all the power humans could devise, they were still infants compared to the unexpected whims of Mother Nature.

In Ty Hale's sector and others along the mighty twin lines facing each other, wind gusts had started blowing. The line of smoke was moved back across the U.S. lines, and that is where many of the bombs were dropped. Ty felt the row of explosions moving his way. He fell backward into his foxhole, and as thick as the dust was and as bitter as the acrid smoke smelled, he could not miss the fact that edges of his foxhole were closing, then opening. Ty and the other soldiers in the ground thought they would be buried alive. The skin of the earth moved in and out at times causing those who could stare up to believe they were being buried alive. It was the War Beast in full arrogance. Then numbness. Numbness throughout.

Centuries passed. Millennia passed. Civilizations and dynasties were only a breath. The hands of clocks either melted or blurred off into space in microscopic pieces. Then from afar came the beginning of a scream followed by the familiar, "Oh, God! Oh, dear God! Medic, medic, medic! Mama, please mama. . . ."

The Cherokee Indian replacement from Tahlequah, Oklahoma, was crawling on his belly away from helping hands. His entrails strung out like bursting snakes spreading his feces on the final pumping of his legs. One arm grasped for Ty, but there was no hand on it. Suddenly his black eyes rolled beseechingly upward straight at Ty Hale and then they were only ancient ink.

The reek of the dead milk cow had moved through Ty's nose to his brain. Partly awake, he stared and tried to remember. He looked across the field at the hedgerow perhaps a hundred yards ahead. The hedges were on each side and behind him as well. He chose the one ahead and started towards it. Somehow he knew death and safety both resided in the entangled branches, rocks, dirt, and roots. His head still had flashes of pain, and nausea came at him in pulsating waves. His legs felt weak but they moved. He wished he had a rifle. He took out the .45. It was only a little comfort, but the short-range gun was all he had. He would make do. Somehow.

His brain tilted toward his younger years no matter how hard he strained to focus on the present. It was somehow comforting to hear the platitudes of his beloved grandfather Jiggs.

"Remember what I told you, Ty. The most lasting laughter should be at our own ridiculous selves."

It was so very clear. They were doing the morning milking; he was a freshman in high school. "You can't borrow yourself out of debt. Always remember that, Ty, and you'll be three innings ahead in life."

His feet lightened a little as this familiar voice filled his battered head. He could see the hedgerow moving towards him. Jiggs's voice moved along with him. "Don't worry, son, we're all living in a world of coincidence."

He was starting his senior year at Lovington High, taken more seriously now because he was blessed with legs that could propel him faster than most others in his state. A neighbor of Jiggs's was running for county judge, and he had wider ambitions. Believing his grandson able to assimilate knowledge through his fast legs, Jiggs had shared a private thought. "It's tough for my old friend to work politics."

"Why is that, grandpa?"

"Well. Well, he's not too well thought of around here. . . . he tells the truth." Even though Ty was young and inexperienced, his legs of genius understood this.

As his thinking took a jump from the flat prairies of Lovington to the mountains and mesas of Las Vegas, he neared the hedgerow.

His thoughts were in the mountains and his body bent low as he neared the hedgerow with the .45 feeling small and pitiful in his hand. Then his thoughts went from the bright blue sky to the blue joyous eyes of Elena. God! How had he not approached her? Held her? Loved her? How could he have been so stupidly reserved? Was it always too much or too little with youth? Her family would have welcomed him as one of their own. They already had. He ached to hold her and apologize. He ached to hold her under any conditions. It was too damn late. Or was it?

The next time he was conscious he was crouched in a foxhole that someone else had dug a few days before. He craved to hear his grandfather's voice again. Actually, any friendly voice would do.

five

e tried to guess when the foxholes had been dug. He shoved his hand in the pile of dirt from the hole. It was only dried about an inch down. They were three days old, maybe. He was aware of something as light as air touching all his body. Oh so slowly his brain told him. The direction wasn't clear yet; but the low rumbling sound that pulsated through the air and earth was the Beast of War clearing its throat, making ready to swallow even more of its sustenance—human blood, bone, and flesh. It was somewhere in the distance.

So now Corporal Hale, lately of both plains and mountains of New Mexico, felt a brief moment of safety. Brief indeed. Somehow in some manner beyond his present ability to recall he had been left behind. Oh, pieces were forming. The blue eyes of Elena had led to the dull permanence of death in her brother's orbs. The past would just have to return as it wished or as it was capable. He had strained sufficiently. He must gather himself into enough of one operating piece of humanity to join his remaining unit. He could hear that eternally voracious beast as a seemingly permanent sound in the distance now. How far away? How would he be able to shoot accurately if he was no judge of distance?

Suddenly Ty laughed aloud. He had no rifle to shoot with. The sound of his laughing voice surprised him pleasantly. Fear receded a moment. He couldn't tell the direction of the great rumbling of thousands of guns firing over such a huge distance. He decided just to move. Movement was the eventual answer to every problem. As long as he moved he lived. And answers and questions and incidents of revelation would come. He had no doubt.

And sure enough, as he crossed the hedgerows he came upon a patch of tall grass where the land was lower and had absorbed more water over the years and the grass had grown tall and had been left uncut.

First he saw the German soldier face down and dark stains where the bullets had exited his gray uniform followed by blood. One hand and a forearm were under him and a "Smessier" short barrel, a "Burp" gun as the G.I.s called it, was still in his other hand. Ty's eyes followed the barrel and led to an American soldier face-down, his M.I. rifle a foot or so from his upturned helmet. Both had been knocked from him as he had taken a burst from the burp gun full in the chest. His shredded pack showed that. Behind and to the side lay another American, his legs and arms widely flung. He had fallen from a burst to the face. Ty's hunting back in Lea County helped him now to read this little battle to the death like the title of a book. Movement must be maintained, he reminded himself. His childhood experiences, his army training, and the recent battles had enclosed his world inside a twenty yard circle, the size of his squad—if there were any left.

Ty grabbed up the rifle from beside the first dead soldier and checked it out. There were three shells remaining in it. He put the untouched helmet on his own bare head, then moved swiftly to the soldier without a face. His pack was undisturbed. Ty was suddenly famished and tore into the pack for food. There were C-rations; the little waxed boxes made his dry mouth almost water. From the body of the dead soldier he took the belt that held the canteen and strapped it on along with an ammunition belt from which two grenades hung. He attached them to his body, drank deeply from the canteen, and crawled over the hedgerows to eat away from the scene of the tiny battle. Tiny? Yes. But as big as the universe to the three combatants. As big and as final as it gets.

He had food and water in his belly. He had a rifle over his shoulder as he headed out. He had ammunition, a pistol, grenades, and a steel helmet on his head. Even though he could not remember how he had arrived at this spot at this instant in time, he knew he was ready to face things as they came. He would keep on moving. Since he was unable to concentrate on the how and why, he would just continue with this moving until—what?

six

Ty was actually enjoying this stroll through the rolling Norman countryside. He had spotted a few farmers doing their chores as they had for centuries. The birds flew about, some tending their nests in the hedgerow brush as well as hunting insects there. The crows cawed, unseen, but one circled in the sky making him think of a New Mexico buzzard. He was watching for an opening or a gate through the hedgerows and finally found a road between them.

He had to face a farmer and ask for water. His canteen was near empty now but his thirst had not been slaked. He spotted a team of workhorses pulling a wagon and an old man and an old woman forking an early crop of hay onto it. He knew they had been unable to gather the hay until now because of the passing violence of many soldiers. The scene stopped him for a moment, and he was torn. Should he go and try talking to them? He probably knew twenty words of French quite well and maybe that many more "somewhats." After the battle across the farmlands and villages he had volunteered to try and find farmers who had survived the passing movement of two deadly armies and barter for milk, eggs, bread, wine, and Calvados that had been hidden from the occupiers. It was need that helped him get the lovely rhythm of the French language, but its singular beauty that had caused him to pick it up so easily. It had become a bit like a favorite song that followed you even to sleep.

He started to go through a gate and talk the best he could to the old couple. He had no worry about his reception. The farmers and their families had always given him respect and all they could spare in food and drink, often refusing payment. But he wasn't ready yet to talk to anyone. He had to walk away from the old couple even though he was deeply moved to see them straining together to make a future no matter how long it had been delayed and how short the time they had left. Beautiful. Nevertheless, he had to have water. Every hundred yards of the road increased his thirst ten degrees. He had no idea which direction he was moving except that constant humming rumble seemed a little nearer. He spotted a large stand of trees to his left and thought there must be water nearby. He looked again as he got closer, peering across an indentation in the rocky hedge.

Zing.

His helmet tilted off his head, and he knew a bullet had removed it. He ducked down and turned the helmet in his hand. There was a deep crease about three inches long; the bullet had broken through a tiny bit and then ricocheted off. The blow caused knives of pain to slice his head, and the nausea tried to return. He fought it to a draw.

From the ancient wars of past lives he had fought in he knew the shooter was in the tallest and nearest tree. Often in retreat the Germans would leave one or more riflemen behind to harass or kill any straggler. Ty didn't think at all. He ripped a dead root from the hedgerow, placed it inside the helmet, and slowly raised the decoy in sight of the shooter.

Silence.

A crow talking. A sparrow chirping. An insect rubbing its wings together. His shallow, forced breathing whistled lightly. Sound. Slight. Light. Split seconds were hours. He had to breathe now. It sounded loud as a church bell. He held his breath again.

More. A tiny bit more. The shooter wasn't falling for one of the oldest tricks in warfare. He must have a scope or binoculars. He would move farther along the fortress fence and try again. Clang. The stick was knocked backwards, but he held on. The helmet rocked slightly on its end and then stopped. He took it in hand. A bullet had made a round, slightly .bent hole in the front and was embedded in the back. The ancient root had slowed it just enough to stop double penetration.

Ty tossed the shattered root across the road, then moved about thirty yards down the hedgerow until he found a patch perhaps twenty feet long where the heavily leaved vines were thick for several inches to a foot above the thick hedge. He raised up and moved along until he could find a small spot to see through. He stared as hard as his eyes could take but he could see no movement in the closest, largest tree except the rustling of the leaves in the slight breeze. But he could feel the shooter in there.

His battle mind and hands went to the two grenades. He unhooked them. How far was it? He tried to imagine the curved turn of the track field or the straightaway of a hundred-yard dash. The tree was about thirty yards away. He jerked the pin, counted to two, and hurled the first grenade in an arc with more force than he thought he possessed. He was reaching for the pin on the second one when the first exploded somewhere in the tree. Leaves were falling. No body. More leaves and a few twigs fell, then he saw a small, leafy limb fall followed by a body, arms flailing the air as if grabbing for a limb, for life, for anything. Then it fell beside the rifle and lay still a moment. In the short time, Ty had raced to a low spot and had the body in the rifle sight. It suddenly lurched to its knees and was reaching for the fallen rifle. Ty shot the body once in the back of the neck. It arched backwards a second and then fell forward motionless.

Ty saw an opening just a few yards down. He walked through and towards the body. He carried his rifle in ready position but knew it didn't matter. He had felt the bullet go into the bone and nerves, shattering it all and killing instantly whatever is called life. He didn't go to view his kill. He went to inspect his canteen for water. It was half full and he drank it all and felt better. He only meant to take a glance at the body but his head and his eyes were jerked to attention. With his rifle butt he rolled the blond head to face the sky.

How could it be his fate to grenade two of these little brain-washed children. My God, this one was younger than the last one. Eleven or twelve. He had read in *Stars and Stripes* how Hitler had established compulsory schools to teach children that there was only one thing to live for, the Third Reich and Herr Hitler, and there was only the same to die for without question or remorse of any kind. He murmured to himself, "How can it be? Where will it lead, this total possession of tender helpless minds turned into seekers of death, even their own?"

He tried to gather hate in his heart for the tiny still figure with his blood feeding the rich Norman soil, the little body that had given its all trying to blow his head off, but tears filled his eyes instead. He hadn't cried since the burial of his parents so far, far back in time. Now he wept for the soul of the world. He bathed himself clean in tears.

He had lost the road between the fields, but lucked into another that edged the southernmost line of hedges. Although the wagon trail moved unevenly because of the different sizes of the fields, it tracked from gate to gates. He saw a fat rabbit leap into a hole under the hedgerow. He stopped dead still as he spotted its mate staring at him through a clump of grass, thinking itself hidden. Its nose twitched, and now and then it bent to take a bite of newly sprouting grass. Where the noon sun caressed its back the grayish brown hair gleamed as if freshly brushed. The sun shined through its delicate ears in a beautiful orange glow. Then his eye caught a movement under the hedge. It was two tiny fur balls of baby rabbits. Suddenly Ty felt that the hedges that decided life and death for human warriors were most of the time protectors and home to countless creatures who lived close to, in, and under the earth. The mother rabbit signaled the babies back into the protection of the hole. Her companion dashed from the clump of grass and disappeared under the hedge as well. The rabbits had ignited that part of him that was a child. He could have shot the rabbits for food. Sustenance. But at this moment he felt only tenderness, grateful for this brief gift of observation. Of quiet peace with a little family. Life.

Now he entered a large grassy field. He could see two cows grazing peacefully a couple of hundred yards away. They were white and contrasted with the blue-green grass and the almost cloudless sky. As he came to the gate out of the large hilly field, a stone farmhouse presented itself. It must be deserted. He could hear no sound of life, not even the visiting of chickens. No dog greeted him. No birds sang. There was an apple tree between Ty and the house. As he approached he stepped on a twig, and it crunched under his foot. He had his rifle handy and ready, but felt a little naked with only the one grenade he had saved. Why? He was as armed as a lone rifleman could be. He could see no reason for fear, but a chill he had never felt before enveloped him like thin ice on a window pane. He hardly breathed. Then he noticed something odd under the apple tree. There were black objects scattered from just beyond the drip line of the outer branches all the way to the trunk of the first tree. He finished his tentative approach and just stood there with only his eyes moving. He could not force them to believe what he was seeing. At last he bent down and picked up a dead blackbird. They were all dead. He examined two more by hand. The sun created a lovely blue and violet sheen on the birds' feathers as he examined them. Unlike humans, who die with their eyes open, seeking the very last gleam of light, the birds all had their eyes closed in seeming contentment. What had caused their demise there in the apple tree where they had stopped to . . . what? Rest? Visit? Hide? Plan their next flight? It was all explained by the large crater he spotted out in front of the house. It was too large to have been made by anything but a railroad gun shell or a bomb. Its perfect roundness told him it was a bomb. There were only a few new leaves from the tree amongst the dead flock of birds. Ty figured they died of concussion. The weirdest, most perplexing element of war was that totally unpredictable force. The birds were all quietly dead and the tree hardly injured. Ty could not imagine why he felt so suddenly, so bitterly how unfair this force had been to the birds. Somehow he knew that he, too, had been a victim similar to the birds, but he had lived. It was silly that he had had a flashing feeling that all this was unfair to the birds. Then he laughed aloud. Where did fairness wedge itself into all this? Any answer at all would do, but none came. His laughter ended as abruptly as it had started. He moved over and stared at the crater, trying to see if any of that implausible concussion was still around. He had the feeling of ridiculousness again.

"Well," grandpa Jiggs always said, "The thing that amazes me the most in all the world is how ridiculous we all are. No exceptions." Then he added softly, "Even so, we're capable sometimes of actually creating miraculous and even beautiful things."

The soothing voice brought Corporal Hale around to doing whatever it was he was meant to do. He saw where the shrapnel from the bomb had half uprooted a tree nearby and shredded the rest in the cluster like a giant saw. A corner of the house was gone, the rocks blown so far away he couldn't readily see them.

All the windows and the front door were gone but he couldn't see evidence of shrapnel striking the house. A barn was flattened except for one corner post to the adjoining corral. A pig hung halfway up, wrapped around the post like a grisly decoration. Beyond, two cows lay dead on their stomachs as if peacefully sleeping. A black horse was stretched out unnaturally beyond them. There was a well house untouched, standing as solid as when the rocks were first fitted together. Senseless, all of it. The sweat had jumped out of his body to the surface of his skin, and a sudden breeze brought back the icy feeling again. He was drawn to the house as he must have been drawn to his mother's breast soon after his birth. His legs had stiffened suddenly and the flint-sharp pain cut at his brain. He was sick and weak, but nothing could stop him. The empty doorway pulled him as irresistibly as gravity. Step by slow difficult step he moved towards it. Slow and steady as a stalking snake.

He hesitated on the large flat rock before the doorway, letting his eyes adjust to the shaded area before him. The simple but strong farmhouse furniture was scattered about in odd arrangements. None of it seemed to be in its proper place in the living room, but nothing was damaged. Some window panes were missing, but he saw no broken glass. He glanced to the side where the front left window of the main room was visible at an angle. The shattered glass was outside, scattered toward the bomb crater when it should have been blown inside. His eyes must be lying, just as his mind had hidden so much from him. He entered, rifle held ready to fire. It seemed that the old wooden floor quivered and sighed at each step. The rag rug was in a pile against the outer front wall. Pictures had been moved from the walls and were lying about the room flat or leaning at odd angles against the walls. The chairs, tables, and sofa were out of place. Awkward. It was taking more out of him than charging a machine-gun position. He leaned against the door jamb into the next room to keep his weakened joints from dropping him.

My God! Someone was sweeping the floor all the way across the room. A woman. A gray woman. Her barren arms seemed to be covered with a green dust as was her expressionless face. She stared at him immobile, the broom unmoving.

He stepped forward with great effort and felt the floor quiver at his effort. He opened his mouth to voice a greeting. It was just as well the sound was contained in his throat for the woman fell to the floor beside the now motionless broom. She stared at the ceiling with dead, dull eyes.

For a moment Ty could not move. He was frozen, it seemed, in place, by the iciness that possessed his being. He had seen too many vacant bodies. There was no use trying to do more. Slowly, with his neck making loud creaking noises shouting into his head, he turned to look through the archway into the next room. A man about fifty-five years old and two teenagers sat ready to dine with their arms on the table. The older man's finger was in the handle of the teapot. To the right a woman bent over a stove, picking up a pot.

In relief, Ty yelled out in his odd French, "Bonjour! I'm an American soldier." He dropped the barrel of his gun to his side and stepped forward as he spoke. "I mean no harm, but I would appreciate a canteen of . . ." The sentence would remain forever unfinished because just as his feet moved through the archway his weight caused the ancient floor to quiver. The man fell face-down on the table and each of the teenage boys fell in different arcs onto the floor. He had tried to accuse his eyes of falsifying their vision, but he could no longer rely on that theory. The three males were as dead as childhood dreams.

Corporal Hale whirled to observe the woman, even moving with almost steady steps towards her. She was still upright at the stove but had fallen with her face in the great pot of potato soup she was preparing to serve her working family.

Without further attempt at thought, Ty pulled her face out of the kettle, and she slipped with great awkwardness to the floor, hitting so hard everything in the house seemed to jar. She lay there with her legs and arms at odd angles and potato soup covering her face, even her eyes. A guilty feeling possessed Ty as if her clumsy fall was somehow his fault. He moved swiftly now. Spying some towels on a rack, he knelt with them and cleaned her face the best he could making sure to close her unseeing eyes. Then he straightened her heavy legs, pulling the skirt down over them carefully. He placed her hands across her breasts and stood up. He started for the archway to escape, but spun about, almost falling, and tossed a salute at the three men and a kiss at the woman on the floor. As he left the house he only saw the woman with the broom as a blurred object. Some neighbor would find them eventually. They would not be missing in action as he no doubt was.

He moved his legs and wished he had the strength to run. He loved to run, but the legs would only move erratically at best. But now his thoughts were being squeezed for answers. Concussion, of course, but how had it gone in the house and blown outward? The picture of all the displaced objects and the perfectly placed corpses was unsolvable for him. For sure a forced blasted in and then back out, creating an instant vacuum. Their breaths were permanently taken by an invisible assailant. Ty Hale pondered uselessly. Clearly there had been a small battle here, a mile or so away, the day before. How had he not heard it? Was his hearing coming and going like his eyesight seemed to be? There was flotsam here. Dry land flotsam: overturned jeeps, burned trucks, and other machinery of war. He could see where the allied tanks had smashed through the hedgerows ahead of the infantry to wipe out the entrenched enemy. There were pieces of bloody German uniforms as well as those of the attacking G.I.s. There were smashed rifles and pieces of battle gear. Fortunately for him, he found enough bloody, shredded belts with canteens attached to drink all he could hold and fill his own canteen. Water was as precious as blood when it was lacking. There was a pack unstained by blood. Only a small shrapnel tear to give it a strange dignity. Ty truly felt it had been placed there for him by the Great-Mystery-in-the-Sky. It had all the proper accoutrements: blanket, slicker, utensils, and a surprising bonus of several packs of Lucky Strikes and two crumpled chocolate bars still in their wrapping. It was loaded and preserved just for him. There were two boxes of C Rations as a bonus. He strapped the treasure on with great thanks to whatever force was responsible and walked briskly until almost dark, not seeing or caring about the landscape right now.

He managed to hide from farmers doing their daily chores and checking on one another's welfare. It was a day to remember—and a day to forget. And that was what he was thinking when he found a medium-sized empty hay barn. He crawled next to a small ble things and dreamed of beautiful things—of blue-eyed Elena Cortez of Las Vegas, New Mexico. He had touched her tenderly all over and she him, and she smelled like fresh roses and violets combined. She tasted like a plum. They were now moving to consummate the delicious preparatory actions when he was suddenly awakened by her cry of abandoned passion, but it wasn't Elena. The gasping cry of pleasure was right here in the barn.

seven

It was as real as Vesuvius. By instinct he felt for his rifle. He had slept without removing the .45. He jerked on his helmet that had the bullet holes both front and rear and moved cautiously around the haystack as the cries were louder and even more gasping. There in the light of the wide open wagon doors a couple fornicated wildly on the thinly scattered hay. The girl's naked legs were above the boy's back as she arched underneath him. He still wore an unbuttoned shirt but was all naked skin otherwise. All she had on was an unfastened brassiere that revealed one firm breast. They furiously finished off the moment of oblivion they had sought. He lay heavily on her, breathing hard. They were teenagers, sixteen, maybe.

Ty was both embarrassed and transfixed. The girl was caressing the man's head when she saw Ty looking at their spent passion. To his astonishment, she smiled up at him and made a little motion to advance. He couldn't help considering her invitation. He instantly ached to possess her freshly used body.

She started caressing the boy's back with her thighs and arching and rotating her middle region again in an effort to arouse her lover. The swiftness she desired was not programmed in the male no matter how young and virile.

Ty turned his eyes away and headed for the door. He walked swiftly outside, breathing heavily and thinking how the day before he had witnessed death in one of its most baffling forms, and just now he had observed the pleasurable act that had brought the dead here in the first place. Though they did not know it, the young around the world were coupling in an effort to replace those dead creatures that were now enriching the earth and fattening worms.

The Beast of War was losing the numerical battle for now, but its conquests could go on forever. The Beast's endurance was insurmountable in the end, but the lusty minds and bodies of the young and smooth were temporary winners. They grappled the world to reach that climax of blindness, of release, birth and rebirth of their own images. Where had these thoughts come from? Ty mused. What was the purpose when he could not even find a few pieces of himself to put together?

He walked on through the hedges feeling a fool for not accepting the most delicious invitation of youth. He stopped and sat in the warm sun. Was it an early August sun? He didn't know or care for a few moments as he ate the last rations from the backpack he honestly felt was blessed just for him. He opened one of the packs of Lucky Strikes and to his surprise, without even thinking, reached in his pocket and found a lighter.

He muttered to himself, "I guess I'm a smoker. Oh well, everyone in foxhole combat becomes a smoker." He coughed as he tried to inhale, but soon adjusted and was relaxed a bit. Hell, why did he have to understand everything that had happened to him in the last few days? He could enjoy nature itself. A yellow butterfly flew jerkily in the morning air. The sun turned its wings a translucent gold for a moment. It was a sight of such beauty he wished the creature had not stopped to feed on the nectar of a small blue flower. But then that had a beauty all its own because the golden flyer would go on and pollinate many flowers that day and give a life of singular beauty in color, in fruit for others. It passed on.

Then a cloud blotted the sun for a second. He longed to hear his granddad's voice amusing and thereby soothing him. He listened for it, but what he heard was digging farther down the hedgerow. All his pleasurable thoughts were gone. The adrenaline of battle surged into his blood and was pumped by the swiftly increasing beat of his heart throughout his body.

The digging was down and on the other side of the hedgerow. He never reasoned at all. It could only be the enemy. He was up, putting his gear together, and forgot about the cigarette. He moved swiftly and as quietly as possible towards the threatening sound. Someone—how many?—was digging in for defense. He couldn't get careless now, not after what he had already survived—whatever that was.

Judging by the sound alone, he decided to risk a peek. He felt he had no choice.

At a low, mostly smooth spot he climbed up the plentiful vine to ease the rifle through. His duty as a foxhole soldier. He was ready to destroy them all. As always, one or the other would perish. This time was the exception. Two farmers of about sixty-five years were cleaning out an ancient irrigation ditch. Ty breathed.

He eased back down to the bottom of the hedge, sure he was making more noise than an attacking tank. He wanted a cigarette, but was fearful they would smell it. To talk to anyone right now was more frightening than the bloody battle he had anticipated. He actually caught himself tiptoeing past the ditch diggers. When the sound dimmed enough he ran. He ran away from two old Frenchmen armed only with picks and shovels.

Although it was not yet noon the sweat poured from him, further smelling up his unchanged clothes. Under the summer heat, the weight of his equipment, and the shocks his body had recently absorbed, Ty lost his ability to run. He even found it difficult to walk. Now he wished again for his granddad to call his spirit back to Lea County as he done before. He needed the soothing voice of Papa J.

He thought of his grandfather and forgot his temporary discomfort. How, he wondered, since Jiggs was a petroleum engineer, had his grandfather developed such a love of reading the world classic novels? Before Ty had lost his parents, he remembered Jiggs taking or making the time to read every evening after the chores were done. Among some of the names Ty remembered were Stendahl, Balzac, Tolstoy, and others, many, many others. The old man loved classical music, too, and would often sit for hours listening to 78 rpm records of Brahms, Beethoven, Lizst.

Ty knew Jiggs only talked about these classics of literature and music with old Dr. Hennly, who was respected all over the area as a good doctor, but was otherwise considered nuts. Those times when the doctor visited Jiggs and they listened to the music were the only moments Mama Jo tolerated alcohol in the house. The two old friends would share a glass or two of bourbon and listen themselves into another world.

One of his grandfather's Wednesday night poker buddies, Josh Peeler, worked in the oil fields. He was a pumper, which meant he drove across the prairies on dirt roads three times a week to the clusters of holding tanks near pumping oil wells and turned spigots on and off to move the oil from a full tank to an empty one. Sometimes Ty was invited to go along on these trips. Peeler seemed to really enjoy his company and the two talked nonstop, mostly about school sports and rabbit hunting. Ty had traveled countless miles on foot and on horseback with his .22 rifle to harvest rabbits for his family's table. Now he thought it would be fun to ride along with Josh Peeler and plunk a rabbit from the comfort of an auto.

He discussed this with Jiggs and was told, "Now son, we can't have ol' Josh Peeler stopping every time you think you've spotted game until his job is over, but late in the day is when rabbits mostly come out to feed." Ty understood. Jiggs went on. "Now son, ol' Josh Peeler is the politest man you'll ever meet. It is a genuine honor to be in his company. He opens doors for everybody. He says, 'No, ma'am' and 'thank you, ma'am' to little girls. He's never farted in public that I've heard or smelled, and he'd choke to death before he'd belch in public. A very proper man, you might say."

Corporal Ty Hale was feeling better already. He felt like running again here in the hedgerows. His grandfather always had filled him full of juice.

Then he broke into a silent smile as he recalled an incident that oil-pumping, rabbit-hunting day so long ago with Josh and Jiggs. Ty's kidneys had started to fill his bladder up so he could hardly hold it.

Finally he overcame his embarrassment and said, "Papa J, I've just got to pee."

"Me, too, son. Do you mind stopping, Josh, so we can water the mesquites?"

Josh slammed on the brakes. As Ty and his grandfather exited the car to relieve themselves, they had company. Josh just crawled right out and stood beside them saying, "I don't need to go, boys, but I'll take it out with you anyway."

"Oh, for joyous joy," Ty could hear that healing voice all the way to France. "Hell, son, everything's gonna be all right. When you get up for breakfast in the morning ninety-five percent of the bad things you think you've got to face ain't gonna happen. Now, where do you find better odds than that?"

The sun, almost overhead now, didn't bother Corporal Hale at all. Something good would happen here, today, where the hedgerows had thinned and the hills and pastures grew larger.

Sure enough, the odds were in his favor. He found a little stream and followed it, drinking in the sight and then kneeling in the water to drink like a cow. He suddenly stopped and thanked Jiggs for his voice and advice as if he was sitting across the dinner table from him. Mama Jo joined them at the kitchen table filled with chicken and dumplings, garden-fresh green beans, and okra. There was a fresh baked chocolate cream pie on the kitchen counter, just waiting to be enjoyed. He was washing the food down with iced tea, and he could hear birds of all kinds singing their conversational songs. The birdsong became real as the creek slowed, deepened, and widened where a few smooth boulders had penetrated the skin of the earth. Ty started taking off his equipment and separating his G.I. pants, shirt, and underwear. He thanked the Great Mystery in the Sky for blessing him with grandparents whose images could travel across oceans in short seconds. The sight of water can do unusual things to a filthy, smelly, thirsty man.

Ty took off his pack and all his clothes except his shorts. He got the cigarettes out to have a quiet moment before he washed his grimy body and clothes. The man who had worn the pack before him had been self-sufficient. He found a bar of soap in the pack, a razor, and a little polished metal mirror. That only added to the fine little surprises the day had already afforded him.

He sat in the thick grass surrounding the pond, smoked, and pondered. It was a long pond, creek-fed, and no doubt held fish of some kind. A mother duck swam out of her hiding place in some reeds followed by seven ducklings. She had no need to worry over them. They turned when she turned and sailed along as if they had tiny motors when she made for some tall grass on the opposite bank. She was feeding on something there and they couldn't grab whatever the mother fed on. Confused, they swam around in ones and twos, watching her every move.

Ty was unaware of it, but he was smiling, thinking that their inborn observational powers would soon allow them to partake of the watery goodies. Those who survived, of course. With the last thought, he could no longer stay out of the water himself. He removed his shorts and stepped in. It was deep enough that he could have dived. The water came right under his chin. He swam about halfway down the creek pond, then back to get the soap. He washed himself over and over with his hands and the bar of hard soap. The water chilled him at first, but soon felt comfortable.

He could put it off no longer. He started soaping and trying to wring the dirt and sweat from his fighting clothes. He wrung them over and over until his arms could no longer twist the durable cloth. Then he spread them on some bushes a few feet from the pond for the sun to finish purifying as they dried.

He looked for a place to rest while he waited for this process to be complete. He found an outcropping of boulders that was partially shaded by underbrush. The rocks had not heated beyond bearing. He got himself a cup of water, propped the mirror up on one of the boulders, soaped his face, and shaved. He paid no attention to the little cuts here and there because he was trying to figure out how many days old his whiskers were. Maybe that number would help him remember the rest of his experience. It didn't, so he rinsed the soap from his face and began replacing everything in the pack. He lay back on the rocks to luxuriate in this moment of cleanliness and the clouds slowly drifting over the one o'clock sun. For just this passing moment he didn't care what had messed up his head and joints. He was so thankful just to be alive, clean, and warm that he dozed off into a half dream. The pond became an island instead of Normandy, and Elena came walking on the water towards him. Her body was as he'd imagined it would be without clothing. She was slim, sinuous, strong, and flowed towards him like the purest sun-blessed water. She smiled and raked her fingers back through her long, dark, gleaming hair.

Then he was awakened by a splash. It wasn't Elena. He opened his eyes and listened to sounds that became softer now. He sat up, looking through the branches, and saw a bare fair-skinned posterior undulating through the water away from him. The woman swam with expert smoothness for a distance and then walked upright out onto the bank where she picked up a towel and started drying herself.

Ty stared in disbelief and then in thankfulness to observe this beauty from such a perfect distance. She couldn't see him and he could see her. The young woman, almost his age, he guessed, carefully dried every part of her curved body with care.

He had a natural urge to leap up and race through the grass to her and . . . what? As she rumpled the towel through her hair the sun caught auburn streaks and turned them nearly red. She pulled on a dress that came just below her knees, straightened it, picked up the towel and hip-swayed away out of sight around a little hillock.

Ty sat upright, rigid, as confused by this apparition of pure beauty as he had been by the house of concussion-dead of the day before. The turn of luck made him laugh aloud once again. He had, even as a baby, been prone to suddenly laugh aloud, often when others were in sober thought. It was something he long ago quit trying to control. Someday in the future, when he finally told Jiggs about the strange happenings of this day, even he-who-believed-in-miracles as simply a part of life would be discombobulated. Ty ignored his confusion and was simply thankful for such a day as this. If he never experienced another damn thing, he would still feel mightily blessed.

eight

Ty dressed. He packed. He checked his weapons, then struck out at a fast walk past the pond, up the hillock. If he followed the little creek he knew he would find this woman of magical beauty. Hell, he must. Something that appealing had to have entered his vision for a reason. But then, maybe she was part of the dream he'd been having about Elena.

The rolling, rich grassland was dotted with a few cows, horses, and a breed of sheep he had never seen, grazing in the distance. Little stands of trees of almost manicured neatness were sprinkled around the landscape. He assumed these clusters were protected to shade domestic animals, wild birds, and game. Clearly these lands had been well tended forever. There was no sign of war here. How could that be?

He suddenly realized how much he was enjoying the introduction to this special part of the earth, which was bringing his mind back to a world of beauty and peace. Even the hedgerows no longer seemed like fortresses. They too had been carefully tended and not too far back in time had been shaped almost like the borders of a great estate.

Then he saw the neat rock barn on the other side of the creek with several corrals made of the same gray limestone rocks. Being from livestock/farm country himself, he recognized these carefully constructed edifices as birthing, feeding and doctoring places for what must be very large holdings, indeed.

He leaned against the cooling rocks of the structure and smoked a Lucky Strike. He carefully stomped it out and covered it with a loose rock. He was ready now to move on to whatever world was meant for him.

At the instant he stepped around the corner of the building, a bird's wing brushed his cheek. He watched in amazement as the small bird, a sparrow perhaps, flew into some trees across the creek. It had never happened to him before. He'd never even heard of such a thing. The touch of the feathers would remain with him forever. It just had to mean something. An immeasurable fraction nearer and his eyeball might have been burst and the bird's neck probably broken.

There was an arched stone bridge across the creek in front of the structures. It was far too big for the creek, but of course, that was in case of heavy rains. There had to be a lot of moisture for the vegetation to prosper so lushly and the little creek to twist so fully and sing so happily.

Ty stopped a moment on the bridge and studied the creek, absorbing its eternally moving water and smooth warm stones without a question marring his jarred mind. Then the question came. Had the woman crossed here, right where he stood? He was sure she had. He could feel the warmth of her footprints penetrating his combat boots.

He moved on now, forgetting his past and the present, and feeling an excitement far beyond his experience at the thought of perhaps seeing this now phantom creature again. He felt the old urge to run, but he only walked, albeit with swift, sure strides for a change. A magic had happened and more was going to present itself. He knew that much. For the moment that was plenty indeed.

The round ancient hills were larger now. He could see them rising in a blue haze in the distance. Just looking at their beauty made him feel whole again, at least for this moment, and moments were huge right now.

The world changed again. In the mid-distance he saw a raptor dive into the valley between two hills, disappear and then show up again farther on as it flew, clutching its prey, towards some trees, where it disappeared to dine unseen. At that instant he heard music. It had to be coming from the hill he was just circling. It was faint at first, and as he increased the speed of his walk it grew louder. The damn questions started again.

The music. It was Brahms. His grandfather was coming to him again. He must be waiting for him beyond the hill. Ty did not know about the movements and orchestration of these classics creations his grandfather loved so much, but he had heard them so often that he had come to recognize Brahms, Beethoven, and Tchaikovsky. This was Brahms. Jiggs had to be nearby, and he surely would regale Ty with some new stories of his poker-playing associates. Ty wouldn't even mind hearing some old ones. He would greatly welcome that, in fact, and sure enough he remembered part of one on his own.

The story went all the way back to World War I, when his grandfather was a captain of infantry somewhere here in France. Was it Verdun? It didn't matter. He never talked to Ty about the machine-gun duels and the killing dysentery, but he did tell him about when he and two of his trench mates had celebrated for three days and nights after the armistice. Oh, it was a long story, but the part that came to him now seemed like a series of clichés. Nevertheless he enjoyed the memory.

"Lieutenant Carver said he had drunk himself bulletproof with the potent Calvados and he had decided he was going to start the war all over again.

"Sergeant Ellis replied, 'Well, I will join you as soon as I have drunk myself invisible.'"

Jiggs also volunteered to join Carver's new army because he was flying about like an eagle and all beneath him would be bombed with bird splatter.

Ty was smiling as the music increased in intensity along with his grandfather's story. He walked around to the far side of the hill just as the Brahms crescendoed to a finale, drowning out the World War I voices.

There before his 20/20 eyesight was a structure of the same gray limestone rocks as the recently observed barn, except this edifice was round. About a quarter of it was wide open, with a wooden porch, where an old man sat changing the record on a Victrola and cranking it by hand just as his grandfather had done.

Ty stood motionless, watching. Off to the side he saw a cluster of buildings around a great two-story stone house. But for now he studied the old man, who had a full head of gray hair, white at the temples, a neatly trimmed mustache and Van Dyke beard, and his wild black eyebrows. The eyes that turned to see Corporal Ty Hale for the first time were full of glowing light like an inner fire.

He stood up as Ty hesitantly approached and asked, "American?"

"Yes, sir," answered Ty.

The old man said, "Welcome," then, "Sit here," and he pointed to one of the several odd chairs on the porch. "And we'll talk after. . . ." and he pointed to the Victrola. He spoke a combination of French and English that reminded Ty of the *Spanglish* spoken in northern New Mexico.

Ty thanked him and sat down. He had already observed that the old man was about his height, five-ten, though Ty judged that he had been much taller before the shrinkage of age. The Brahms piece was building now. Ty felt embarrassed holding the rifle across his lap. As the volume of the composition increased, so did the weight of the weapon. He slowly leaned it, stock down, off the porch and resumed his listening position, hoping he had not disturbed the old man's obvious pleasure. Soon, Ty was caught up in the magisterial rendition.

Every now and then the old man would raise his arms and conduct, briefly smiling at Ty as if they alone shared the secret of the Holy Grail. The face of his grandfather melded with that of the old man, and Ty closed his eyes to hold that vision. He suddenly felt a kinship with the old man, and then he, too, became as lost in the recorded performance as he was from the explosion that had twisted and muddied his mind.

When the record stopped, they both remained still for a moment. Then with surprising agility the old man stood and moved to Ty with his hand out.

"Please, forgive me. I am Phillipe Gaston. This is my home." He swung his arm in an arc taking in everything in sight. "I see you have a feeling for Brahms. And you, Corporal?"

"I'm Corporal Ty Hale of the United States Army, sir. Pleased to meet you." They shook hands and Ty continued, "He is one of my grandfather's favorites. I've listened with him, my grandfather, as far back as I can remember, but I'm certainly no connoisseur."

"Ah, I see, but you listen with your heart. I can tell."

Ty was embarrassed at his lack of conversational knowledge of the great composer and blurted out, "Monsieur Gaston, I . . . I am lost."

"From your unit?"

"Yes, sir, but it's more than that. I'm lost here," and he spread both hands around his head. Then Ty realized he still wore the helmet with the bullet holes in it. There was no question now. Phillipe Gaston was a true gentleman. He had probably noticed the bullet holes in the borrowed helmet instantly, but had made no remark.

Ty removed the helmet, blushing and stammering. "I . . . I found myself . . . that is . . . I woke up with no rifle, no helmet. This one I took from a body. One I stumbled upon. I. . . ." He held the helmet in his hands, spinning it around awkwardly, and then placed it on the porch by his rifle.

Phillipe Gaston looked away across his hills and pastures for a moment of deep concentration, then back at Ty. It was obvious he had reached some kind of conclusion.

"Well then, there is something you must do, Corporal Hale. You shall be our guest for as long as you like. Then, I'm sure you'll find that which is lost. Here. I'll play us some Beethoven," he said softly as he proceeded to change the record. "Crank the machine."

Ty was overcome with emotion. All he could do was collapse, speechless, in the chair. Gaston sat down beside him, saying in his strong, velvety voice, "Let us rest, my son. It will soon be wine time."

And so they did. Ty sat in a pleasurable trance and felt the touch of the feather stronger than before.

Gaston said, after a while, "Of course, for maximum effect Beethoven should be played to the fullness of sound, but for now. . . ." Ty had already noticed that Gaston left many sentences unfinished except in his own mind.

The movement came to an end. Gaston arose and said softly, "Please, come with me, Corporal," and he walked towards an open archway into a round room.

Ty followed and was amazed to see how much bigger it was inside than his cursory glance from outside had suggested. There were rows of benches, each elevated above the other, leading downward to a stage. A man sat at a piano there. A natural light from a carved glass opening in the ceiling illuminated him as if he were under a spotlight. He was bent over the piano working on some sheet music. Ty and Gaston were all the way to the stage before he noticed them—such was his concentration. The man was somewhere between 35 and 40 years of age. He was delicate of build and face except for a very high forehead where his hair was far back but thick and bushy, not unlike a lion's mane.

He stood to face them, bowing ever so slightly.

Gaston said, "Corporal Hale, meet Hans Heinike. He was once a student of mine. He is a pianist and an arranger of the . . . superior music."

Hans spoke in French with only a slight German accent. "I am always a student of Maestro Gaston." He shook Ty's athletic hand with his delicate one, displaying surprising strength and looking into Ty's eyes as if he could see musical notes written there.

"It is my pleasure, young man."

"Thank you, Mr. Heinike. It is good to meet you, sir."

Hans said, smiling, "Only he," waving a gesture at Gaston, "is a Sir. Please, I am just Hans."

Ty's eyes were on the sheet music where Hans was creating his own arrangement of Mozart. Ty reread the name with disbelief. How could it possibly be? His grandfather, way back in the flatlands of Lea County, had introduced him to the superior music in the same order as Gaston was doing now: Brahms, Beethoven, and Mozart. They were also Jiggs's favorites.

"Hans, come. It is wine time," Gaston said as he led them to the porch and arranged chairs, signaling them to sit.

Ty was facing the great gray almost-white stone compound, when the woman-of-the-pond appeared with a tray of various cheeses and biscuits and two bottles of wine. Her movements awakened his memory. He touched his cheek where the bird had brushed him lighter than a turtle's breath. Her body walked in a slow dance of various ancient rhythms right to the table. As she set the tray down, her smile and her large green eyes rendered Ty temporarily helpless.

Renée, the only child of Phillipe Gaston and the late Eva Gaston, was introduced to Ty. He shook her warm, soft hand in pleasurable deceit. They had already met without introductions at the pond of destiny.

Gaston poured the white wine, apologizing that perhaps Ty would have preferred red. Since he was no connoisseur, he assured his host that his appreciation of the drink was great. In fact, his gratitude was beyond appreciation. A few hours ago he had been covered in dirt, sweat, and blood splatters. Here he sat, bathed, with a glass of wine on a porch surrounded by lush green pastures in the company of three of the most intriguing people he had ever met or even dreamed of meeting. But the thing that was the most incredible was how welcome and at ease he felt even before the wine had worked its grape-borne spell.

Gaston held his glass out in a toast. The four of them touched glasses.

Gaston said, "Destiny smiles on all of us alike, so here's to destiny!"

"To destiny!"

They talked of music and books and things that last, of gardens, of livestock, especially horses, which they all admired.

By sunset they had emptied the first bottle and made a good start on the second. Ty was in a mood of relaxation he would never have believed could befall him again. In all their conversations they had asked him nothing personal. Only the most cultivated and worldly could have such an understanding. However, they were not so careful of their own lives. As the day eased on, Ty picked up many things indirectly.

Gaston was still in quiet mourning for his late wife, Eva, who had been an internationally known singer of popular songs. She was buried on the hill above the porch, towards the setting sun.

Renée had just started her studies at the Sorbonne and voice studies with her mother. She had hoped for a career singing with her mother. But the war, always the war, had trapped them all. She had managed to get free to come home because of the popularity of her mother and the fame of her father. It had been two years since Commandant H. Eubank and his staff had taken over Château Gaston. The family of three and their remaining servants, Nicolas and Marie Didot, had been kept on as free-roaming prisoners of the German army.

Hans had been a student, the most promising that maestro Gaston had ever had. The rest of his story remained a mystery to Ty.

Grandfather Jiggs was still very much on Ty's mind. As sophisticated and talented as Ty had found Gaston to be in this short visit, his own grandfather was Gaston's equal in many ways. The voice came to him in the midst of this rare evening.

"Time, timeless time," Jiggs was saying, "Time by the clock, time by the calendar are only illusions to give a semblance of sanity to the human animal. If you are looking down the barrel of a gun that is held by a killer, a split second becomes years. My son, if you were waiting for the foreclosure to be served on your home the preceding hours would also become years. Every creature you see on this earth with the possible exception of the cockroach was something else millions of years ago maybe ten, twenty, one hundred and fifty million years ago. Ninety-eight percent of those who were here just a short time back in geologic history are gone, gone, gone, lost in that invisible force we call *time*. Enjoy these moments now, son. Time is only useful as a word. Forget the thought. Live. Enjoy."

He welcomed Jiggs's silence now as much as he had appreciated the sound of Jiggs's voice in his head. Ty was afraid he might seem distant and disrespectful to his hosts. So now he freely talked of the grandparents who had raised him on a stock farm amid the vast cattle ranges. He told how Jiggs had edged him into reading the European classics and passed on his love for the classical music that was obviously the very breath of Gaston and Hans and possibly Renée. He revealed, smiling, the other side of his grandfather who enjoyed the camaraderie of his drinking, hunting, and poker-playing friends. People who have worked with their hands hold the upper and lower parts of the world together.

Ty talked of the fine things his grandparents had exposed him to, and how lucky he was, for without those revelations from music and words he would not be enjoying himself so much as he was right now. His candor was all he had to bring to the conversation, so he waited for their reaction with some dread. He need not have worried. They laughed in understanding, and they laughed because it was all part of feeling good together in these moments.

Finally, Gaston said, "This man of many interests, your grandfather, is someone I'd like to know." The others nodded in agreement. Oh, they had been special, these moments.

There was the lighting of candles and the pouring of the last glasses of wine as the sun left the great sky. Ty had been trying not to look at Renée too long, but now he could not help himself. The one-fourth share of two bottles of fine wine and the ease of this new companionship relaxed him. He openly admired the wide-set green eyes that seemed to laugh over her moist, full blown lips. Those eyes were so direct and open to everything. His appreciation of her natural beauty and instant wit was growing by the moment.

Ty became aware as the sun went down that the seemingly slow movement of light from the horizon into the early night sky was pulsating with the lights from artillery duels. Night fire from hundreds and hundreds of cannons could be seen and then later heard in a whispering rumble. Silence at the wine table. Then the same illumination arced upward far to the left with smaller arcs of light in between.

Silence still held at the table of four.

Then. Then the thin skin of the earth rippled in revulsion across the hills down through the valleys of Château Gaston's pastures and under the porch, where their feet told their minds of the mighty forces creating death over such vast distances.

Gaston spoke first. "Ah, Marie will have our dinner ready to serve." They all followed him the fifty yards to the great arched entryway to the château grounds. Gaston held the door open for all of them. Ty touched Renée's back to guide her ahead of him, and they both felt the touch as sure as the great war had shaken the earth. His war. Her war. Their war. Everybody's war.

nine

The Didot family had been serving the Gaston family for hundreds of years, and Marie and Nicolas Didot were the last in the line. Before Hitler, there were at least a dozen Didots tending cattle, sheep, pigs, orchards, gardens, vineyards, horses, goats, fowl—a seemingly endless parade of pets, service animals, and farm produce. Throughout those centuries the Gastons had dined and played well largely through the dedication and skill of the Didots. In turn, generations of Gastons had paid the Didots properly and given them family-like love and respect. The war had left only the two sixty-year-olds. So was the lineage of Philippe Gaston and his daughter, Renée. Everything changes or ends. No one ever has a choice—although most think they do.

The Didots looked somewhat alike—stocky, strong of leg, and pleasant of face. However, her face was round with gray eyes of iron will, and she still showed signs that she had been pretty when younger. He had a broken beak of a nose and the same gray eyes as his spouse. He moved with the stiffness and muscularity that come from years of hard labor. They liked to work. It was their life, their purpose. So during the invasion of General Eubanks and his large staff, they did double duty as a matter of course. It would be more appropriate to say triple duty. All the tending of plants and animals during the day, the cooking, sewing, and cleaning up after dinner allowed them little solid sleep during their short nights. It was the way of the richly blessed and their servants. It had always been so. It might seem to change, but in the end only the implements and methods would be different.

Ty would soon know all this, but for the moment he was in a place he had never been, with total escapist joy. The wine was served and then the roasted lamb, and bread the likes of which he had never feasted on. Its soft inside and crisp crust enhanced all the rest of the food. In Ty's thinking, it would have been a feast by itself. It wouldn't matter if all the best food of all the different lands of the world had been served, he was feasting on the words of Gaston and the totality of Renée.

In spite of the pleasures of eating, drinking, and conversation, the war invaded their camaraderie and stilled the magic as they retired to the massive great room, wide enough to play tennis in, with a ceiling three stories high. At a later date Ty would spend much time studying the old oil paintings, the ancient armor. For now just the scent alone, of centuries of love, death, and desire, was spellbinding.

They sat around a low table drinking brandy. The young had now found comfort side by side. The wide-ranging conversation filled the château with voluble magic. Hans had dropped his attempt to draw a musical picture for the table. Then he tried again, attempting to describe how a short series of properly arranged notes could give a modern scope to a Beethoven movement that he swore was as large as any modern battle. He changed subjects abruptly. His delicate hands drew words in the air and then he voiced a descriptive comparison that seemed to satisfy him,

"If bacteria were the size of the average human being then a soccer ball would be bigger than the earth." This was accepted all around.

Then Gaston pondered aloud a surprising analysis of war, the essence of it possibly inspired by his very own best protégé,

"Oh, dear ones, war is such a short word for such a massive infectious entity. War is a beast that forever roams the earth seeking out the evil and vainglorious to spew on and inject its incurable poison. This deadliest of all entities can break off part of its many interlocking and forever moving parts, as it deposits its eggs which will eventually hatch into patches of war, or continents of war, or worlds of war as here right now. When those die out, war is like some lizard whose tail, or parts thereof, can be destroyed and shortly grow back making the beast whole and as powerful and eternal as gravity."

They, the chosen four companions here in the great room, absorbed Gaston's words like a drop of sweat on a new sponge. Their minds reeled into their own words.

Renée said, as though to herself, "Someday, of course, humans will no longer exist on this planet."

Ty said, almost exuberantly, "However, it will then all be meaningless because there will be no one for the last survivor to tell it to."

Before anyone could reply, he let his shoulder touch Renée's for a brief moment and thought to himself that there was an unknown presence about her like moon shadows. And then the thoughts of maestro Gaston became words that Ty could hear again.

"Well, dear," Gaston said speaking to his daughter directly, "when the war entity has depleted the human race, it can then start in creating a contamination that will thrust species against species in bitter and savage battles. The joy of battle is endless to War. We might as well relish the times it is in hiding."

"Like now," murmured young Ty Hale, "like this golden moment right now," and he hoisted his brandy glass in gracious glee. All joined in.

Gaston then poured more brandy for all and motioned them to the cavernous fireplace above which hung a fine portrait of

Eva silently singing her soul into the room, into the world of disgrace. Gaston was playing the violin for his love in the painting's background.

"God, she was enchantingly beautiful," Ty said to himself. He was overheard by Renée, who squeezed his forearm for a second and said in her strong but soft voice, "Yes. Yes, she was. Thank you."

They all four knew what to do as the silent thought encircled them. All raised their glasses to the image of Eva and said in clear, respectful voices, "To Eva. Forever."

Ty put his hand on Renée's and whispered, "Forever is a long time." Their night of nights was done.

twelve

omorrow. Tomorrow was just another word for hope. You
don't really know what you've lost until it's vanished forever. Who is that lovely nude girl swimming away, away,
away? Blue eyes of Elena, blue skies of Normandy, blue shadows
and lights on the blackbird's wings. Hold me, Renée. Hold me
all over. Just like that. Come closer, Papa J. I can't quite hear you.
Ah yes, now I hear you clearly. Is it all just custom or coincidence,
grandfather? But I saw water running uphill. Closer before you
speak again. Come closer. I want to tell you about this woman
Renée. She is painted on the canvas of my soul.

The pineapple grenade is the rifleman's dessert. He shares it
with many of the enemy. The 88s are wailing in the sky like lost
children zzzzztt bang. That one is now laughing. It found its destiny and that is me. I'm trying to pull the pieces of myself together,
but some are too small. Even so I'm partially back together. I can
walk now. I can't quite run yet. If I can just find one more piece
of me, I'll be able to run again. I love running. Ahh, I've been
wasting this effort. The metal pieces of the 88 found others. It
was that force, the shrapnel-throwing force, that picked me out.
My mistake again, Papa J. It was a bomb. A big bomb. One of
our own, I think. I don't know. Where is Renée? I want to tell her

something. Something very important. I must ask her questions. There are mysteries here at Château Gaston. Many, many mysteries. It is as if Château Gaston has replaced my mind.

Corporal Ty Hale knew there was light. The sun peeked over the eastern hills and pierced the bedroom through the nineteenth-century glass window. He felt his face. It was him all right. He had often seen it while shaving. He was in a feather bed. Duck-down feathers. Soft. So very soft. He dozed a moment and then continued his discoveries.

Ty opened his eyes. He slid up in the bed and looked around. It wasn't a dream now. A closet door was open and several sets of shirts and pants hung there, and underwear, but no army-issue anything was visible. His uniform, rifle, and backpack were gone. On the large elegant water basin were toiletries. It was too much to absorb. All he could have wished for after a few weeks of sleeping on dirt, surrounded by dirt. Foxhole dirt was the bed. All these luxuries his eyes revealed were too much for a down-in-the-dirt rifleman. Only the greatest of heroes deserved such as this.

There was a light knock on the door. He pulled the tightly woven sheet up under his chin and ventured, "Come in."

Renée entered, carrying a tray with eggs, bacon, fruit preserves, the wonderful bread, and a ceramic pot of coffee. Beautiful Renée. She could have been the reincarnation of Nefertiti or Cleopatra. Her scent seemed to come from all the baths, perfumes, and natural secretions of all the chosen princesses throughout history. Her thick auburn hair was again in a long pony tail that tossed over her shoulder hanging over one breast to emphasize their exact right proportions. Nothing could have been more beautiful.

Ty Hale started trying to talk. He choked and coughed embarrassingly and finally saying, "This is too much . . . please."

The tray was secured in his lap. She put her fingers to his lips to silence him, leaned over and kissed him on the cheek. The touch of feathers again.

She straightened up, saying, "Take your time. Come down later. I have put your uniform and equipment away for now."

He wanted to grab her and pull her under the covers with him. It both hurt him and warmed him to see her exit the room tossing the pony tail as she sent him a smile of possibilities.

When he had recovered a little from her powerful presence, he ate, he drank, he lived. *My God*, he thought, *I live.*

His grandfather's voice came into his brain. "My boy, all things that happen in your life, the things you think are miracles, will become commonplace to following generations. On and on, you see. However, one must accept these little miracles in full faith and pleasure no matter how brief. Sometimes they last a. . . ." The familiar voice faded away. He must arise and pass again through the golden door of *the present.*

eleven

Renée's green eyes warmed as she saw how much Ty was enjoying the tour of the farmyards. The sounds and smells of pigs, chickens, and ducks reminded him of home and warmed his heart.

The horse barn was long and clean with the scent of new hay. There were many empty stalls, but Nicholas was tossing feed to seven or eight animals. There were at least three pleasure horses— two Arabians and one a mixture Ty couldn't figure out.

Renée sensed his curiosity. "He's a thoroughbred walker. That was the General's horse. He rode it at least twice a week."

"General?"

"General Eubank, the invader of the Château Gaston for almost two years." For a moment her green eyes flashed a kind of fire Ty had not seen before.

They moved on through the double-sided horse barn out through a gate to a large round rock corral. Ty surmised it was the principal equine training ground. Like everything else it had obviously been built to last for centuries.

Renée moved forward. It was her domain. Ty followed except when he was opening gates for her. He was full of curiosity, but his grandparents had taught him that it was impolite to ask personal questions. Other probings, the kind that would enhance work, productivity, and such, were all right.

Ty's imagination was hard at work. He felt strongly that Hans was a deserter from Hitler's army, and the permanent absence of Eva Gaston intrigued him. Something was terribly amiss there, he was sure.

Ty suddenly felt foolish having these thoughts. Why was he worrying about these things? Truth was, he felt so good at this moment that he laughed out loud. Renée gave him a wide smile, but she managed to hold back her natural questions. This consideration pleased Ty even more, and he chuckled again.

They walked along the creek. Meandering beside the stream gave him an opportunity to observe Renée without being obvious, or so he imagined.

She wore a pale rosebud-dappled dress. It was not tight, but whatever material it was made of got his blessings for she walked in that flowing stride he had noticed at the pool when he first saw her. It clung to her and gave Ty a picture of her body that would have made the great figure painter Reubens slaver. If he had known how to keep it hidden Ty would have slavered a bit himself.

She squatted by a small pool formed by a natural dam of rocks and pointed. "Look! Trout."

He bent beside her and strained to see. He could only see rocks and pebbles under the slowly swirling water.

"See?" She took his hand, extended his trigger finger, and put hers against his. "Look, Corporal Hale, you are shooting an M.1. Sight your finger like a rifle and look just above."

It worked. He could see the lovely lined trout. They moved swiftly in jerks, feeding where the water hit the bank.

"I see them." He closed his hand on hers and squeezed gently.

The pressure was returned. He carefully pulled her around on her knees to be even with him and pulled her body against his. On the way to her slightly open lips, he glanced at her eyes. They were closed. As he tasted her lips, her being, his eyes closed and he floated a long time bathed in a special sunlight.

Then they sat quietly for a spell. There were no words. Before they moved on, he knelt by the spot where he had sighted the trout at last and said, "Thank you, fish. Swim sweetly."

She was smiling at Ty as they locked hands and walked on. Ty smiled at the entire universe, still not thinking, but wondering at his boundless luck. They sat on a hillock and looked across the lush meadow below the creek.

"I'm the luckiest bastard still living," he said. He didn't even have to think about it.

They sat with their hips touching in the grass so when she turned to glance at him he felt her green gaze.

"Luck," she said, "Luck is sometimes called a blessing. And a blessing is often called luck."

He stood up, pulling her with him. "Well, I have both then, don't I?"

"You, my darling, will always have my blessings."

They walked down toward the pool, and he glanced sideways at her elegant profile and hugged her around the waist. She reciprocated.

At the pool, she pointed up a hundred yards and said, "That's where I first saw you sleeping. Your uniform was drying on the bush."

He broke his lifetime of rules and asked her, "You saw me?"

She smiled shyly.

He asked, "And what did you think?"

"That you were a soldier who had temporarily deserted the horror. And then for some reason I thought . . . no, he's lost. And, of course, I was right as always." Then, laughing, she moved down to the pool shedding all her clothes as she went. She stood for a moment at the very edge of the enchanted water. Her back arched above the curve to her solid rounded buttocks. Her breasts thrust out as if she'd suckle the world. The world stopped on its axis. He would never forget this moment. Renée was a living sculpture, a magnificent portrait. Then she was in the pool swimming away from him and as swiftly as he could disrobe he dived into the pool and swam until he was under her. If he'd been able to breathe water he could have stayed there swimming on his back until the pool dried up.

He came up beside her gasping in air. They both headed for the bank.

Renée grabbed her clothes and held them around her until she reached a place to sit down. They stretched out on the rocks side by side, breathing hard. The August sun was just past noon and it baked them pleasurably dry. They reached and touched each other at the same moment and moved in between the rocks to a moss-covered swale. They joined ever so naturally, together in a honeyed vacuum.

Ty stopped trying to analyze his recent confusion. He was enjoying this unexpected gift of life too much. He pitched in and almost gleefully helped Nicolas Didot with some of his chores. The milking and feeding of livestock were familiar activities.

He was pleased to learn that some neighbors who pastured their cattle and sheep at the Gastons' helped out occasionally. They shared in the profits and meat for the table. These two families, the men, their wives, and children from six to fourteen years old, eased the burdens of the Didots.

Almost everyone in Normandy had suffered many hardships during the Nazi occupation, but the Gastons were the exception, because General Eubank was enraptured with Eva's voice. He was also in awe because she had sung for Hitler. Eva had not even known that Hitler was present at the performance. The S.S. had installed Hitler and his staff in a veiled balcony so slyly that none but the manager of the great hall was aware of his presence. Philippe accompanied her with his violin, giving up the teaching and performing of the classics to share the popular music performances she so excelled in.

"Anyway," Renée said, as she explained this to him, "everyone was astounded that Eva could sing so touchingly with a only a solo violin for accompaniment. The promoter of the concert had asked my mother to sing one of Hitler's favorites, "The Merry Widow.' She did. They were trying to survive."

Renée looked at Ty in exasperation and continued, "If my mother had known Hitler was present and it was *his* request for the song, her throat would have closed and she would have died right on the spot. And you know the gossips? Word got out. Not even the S.S. could keep it quiet. She was the famous Eva Gaston who had sung for Hitler, even though underneath she was deeply hurt, both by those who admired her and by those who hated her for the same innocent night of song. This evening of a beautiful performance would ultimately take her life. It did save our family's way of life, at an unimaginable price. The German Army respected General Eubanks enough to honor his wishes to leave us alone while he was a *'guest'* at our estate."

Ty was stunned by all this information, and equally stunned that Renée was willing to share it with him so soon. Parts of the puzzle were still missing, but his childhood training kept him from asking further questions.

As the days passed, the two young people made love wherever they could find a private place. A bond far beyond the flesh united them. They had made love in horse-barn hay and between rows of green beans in the garden, but Renée refused to make love in a bed.

Once when he asked her to come to his room, she took both his hands and locked her green eyes on his brown ones, saying, "Please, my darling, we cannot do that until I know it's permanent . . . and that has nothing to do with either one of us."

Corporal Ty Hale of Lea County and Las Vegas, New Mexico, questioned her, but not aloud. He almost had one of his laughing spells when he wondered who in the hell it did concern if not the two of them.

He stifled the laughter and followed her down the hall and out into the courtyard. She was leading him to explore something new. They were on their way to see something she called a great secret.

They wound down a curved pathway, several feet wide, to the Gaston compound church. It was hidden by the curve of the tall green hedgerows on each side. The chapel was stone, just like everything else, but was painted white as a new cloud. He should have been surprised at its size and elegance, but he was long over that around the Château Gaston.

She knelt for just a moment before a magnificent silver-cast statue of the crucified Christ hanging in space by what appeared to be silver chains, muttered something, crossed herself and said to Ty, "Now, I'm going to show you how the Gastons have survived here for so many centuries."

She moved to one side of the pew and taking hold of two sides, she twisted it halfway around. There was a noise of rollers working smoothly, and the floor behind the pew disappeared, leaving a hole where stone steps descended.

She started down the steps. "Come on, soldier, follow me."

He did. At the bottom of the stairway there was an anchored iron rod with a handle of about eighteen inches folded against the wall. She opened a cabinet built into the wall. By the dim light, she took out a box of matches and lit the large candles in the niches. She handed one after the other to Ty. Then she pulled the handle out on the iron rod and moved it sideways. The rollers moved again and the portion of the floor that had first opened now closed smoothly and perfectly into place. Not a ray of light came through. She took one of the candles from him and moved on ahead.

There was a long passageway perhaps eight or ten feet wide with rooms on each. At the second opening, with a cloth hung door, she entered. He followed. There, on ancient iron pegs driven expertly into the stone walls, Ty saw his uniform hanging above his pack and rifle, which leaned against the wall. Beside his hung another uniform. A German one.

At his questioning look, she said, "Hans. He deserted from the fortifications at Omaha Beach."

"I was there. I'm glad he was gone. One of us might have shot the other."

"Well then, we're happy for all of us," Renée said.

"When? How long was he gone before we invaded?"

"I don't remember exactly. General Eubanks and his staff were still here. Months anyway. Hans hid in the conservatory, where he had studied and worked with father several years ago."

"How on earth did he ever escape detection?"

"That's another miracle." She sounded relieved. "My father started taking before-dinner walks until the general's guards became used to it. Finally, he got a hand-drawn map to Hans. Hans circled around and somehow avoided detection until he got into the church. The other miracle was the fact that he could follow directions well enough to open the stairway. I don't know how long he lived down here. It seemed like forever to all of us. Nicolas was responsible for most of the contact and supplying him with milk and other needs. There are two other entrances or exits. I want you to know where they are. I feel you should, okay?"

"I would appreciate that very much," he answered, thinking that he might just have dire need of this haven before long. Then he cut those thoughts off. He followed on past several more rooms where flour, cornmeal, and other supplies were stored in metal containers to keep them safe from rodents. Then Renée pointed out a narrow rocked-in tunnel between two rooms. "This is perhaps a quarter mile long and opens into thick brush and plants concealing the exit completely. We'll use it."

He was amazed when she secured a sizable key from a hidden spot and used it to open a large wooden door braced by iron strapping. He was again pleased to see how easily the massive door swung open. The Gastons kept even ancient hideaways in fine condition.

The candlelight revealed a wine cellar worthy of royalty. There was no showing off, no braggadocio about Renée as she handed bottles to Ty, explaining as if she were counting the days of the annual wheat harvest. "Mouton 1890. It was a very special year for the grapes."

On and on, she recited names he had never heard before, years as far back as the 1700s. Then there was a long section of brandies, cordials of all kinds, and even a row of the fiery Calvados. He wished he could remember these names and dates but knew they were too varied for him ever to recall. He quit trying. He had suddenly caught himself thinking he would be here at Château Gaston his entire life. "My God," he muttered. He'd only been here—what? six days? seven? eight? It seemed immeasurable suddenly. He was following Renée, that's all. She pointed out a room of cots that would bed down an entire platoon of infantry—and probably had more than once. She pointed out the drinking water. It was supplied by gravity through an underground spillway. There was even a toilet that would have made the ancient Romans proud. He wondered if the Romans had installed it.

Suddenly Renée turned to him and cupped his neck in her free hand. She kissed him like the touch of a feather and said, in a voice softer than a sparrow's breath, "You see, my darling, you'll be safe here at Château Gaston as long as you live."

He reached for her waist with his free hand but she was already turning to move to the escape tunnel and lead him down the curving stone to the exit. She knelt, pinching out the flames of their candles. He followed her through a jagged opening by natural light, and there was the vegetation she'd mentioned covering the exit. Renée started pushing the growth to both sides. She was struggling.

Ty moved to help her. "Let me have the honor of doing something for you."

At last they were out of the grappling vines. They stood in a grassy ten-foot indention in the earth. Without a word, they drew together and fell to the cushioning grass. Only the Great-Mystery-in-the-Sky and a pair of casually flying crows would know they were spliced into oneness.

twelve

There was a lot to celebrate. The son and daughter of the Didots had made it home alive, thin but in good health. Claude, the thirty-five-year-old son, had a new wife, Marcelle, who had been raised on an estate in Brittany and knew her way in that world of the earth and its domesticated animals.

The daughter, Molina, thirty-two and born and reared at Château Gaston, was no less welcome even though she was four months pregnant and not married. She swore the father would be here as soon as the Resistance no longer needed him. To celebrate the prodigals' return, Renée was preparing to go to the house of the Didots with a fruit cobbler made by her own lovely hands.

The general and his staff, on their sudden departure, were forced to abandon, in addition to a generator and a good deal of food, a shortwave radio, which Phillipe understood how to operate. He followed the progress of the Resistance and the war news in general. But the return of the Didot children so soon was unexpected great news. Now he could really devote himself to his protégé, Hans, the honored deserter. Ty was aware of their work no matter where he was on the château grounds. He could hear notes and scales being tested and now and then a complete performance with Hans on the piano, Philippe on the violin. His pleasure in this music was puzzling to the soldier. He thought himself musically deficient, but he delighted in others being able to play so beautifully. So by an irresistible urge he was drawn to the round house where the musicians were working on a Mozart piano concerto.

Ty sat on the edge of the porch and absorbed the mid-afternoon sun like a bear emerging from hibernation. It crossed his mind that the August sun would be hotter than a furnace to the men who were firing and dying twenty or thirty miles away. He dismissed this thought. The music coming from the round house made him think of home and his grandparents. He fell into a reverie.

He could hear his grandfather's soothing voice enter his half-consciousness. "*Ty, my boy, I've been trying to connect with you for over an hour. There is a lot of local news, but the one I wanted you to know was Marvin Ake. He lives about five miles south on the old Tatum highway. You remember him? Here we go about 'time' again. Marvin's little sashay brings it to mind. You hear me? Good. We're some little distance from Normandy. Time is simply decided by what you're doing. Enough of that for now. Well, ol' Marvin called yesterday and said he'll be turning one hundred. Said the county newspapers were sending some people out to interview him. He was scared to death and so was his sixty-year-old widowed granddaughter; she lives and works on the family stock farm. They needed company, friendly company, so I went over and messed around drinking coffee and a shot of bourbon with Ake before the reporters got there. They asked him a lot of questions about the supposedly Wild West of his youth, but mainly they wanted to know what he thought had contributed to his long life. Well, I thought he would tell them he had chocolate cake for dessert after every dinner for sixty years, or for sure that he enjoyed one double shot of bourbon each day for as long as he could remember. They couldn't get this part out of him, but kept pressing anyway. Ol' Marvin thought and thought, then finally he told 'em, 'Well, hell, somebody's got to get up early and feed the hogs.' That's ol' Marvin Ake, all right.*" Jiggs chuckled on but faded away back across oceans and prairies to New Mexico.

Ty was listening to the music again when he heard a droning. The sound slowly grew stronger. Then he looked up past the cloudless sky and *saw* the sound. The mighty fortress bombers, maybe eighty or a hundred of them, moved slowly, inevitably, like the turning of the horizon. The fighter plane escorts were tiny as mosquitoes accompanying flying elephants. "They are going to kiss Berlin good-bye." Philippe stood beside Ty on the porch. The pristine blue sky enveloped destruction beyond any known heretofore, tons and tons of bombs being carried overhead in perfect formation. The nearness of the unknown caused chill bumps on Ty's neck. He jerked his head away from remembering something, a memory he desperately wanted to experience. Dejà vu was blown to bits again.

Philippe sat at the table, soon joined by Hans, then Ty. "Berlin is being attacked by the British, the Americans and many others," said Philippe, "all moving from the ground and sky to fall upon the ruins. The Russians are closing in. Before long the vise will be ready to close completely."

Hans looked at the maestro. He knew that Philippe had mixed thoughts, memories of love and fear, music and death that had filled his last years in Berlin. He had met Eva there. She could sing in French, English, and German, and was doing all three in one song in a beer garden. There was so much to remember and now more to forget.

Hans, a Berliner by birth, sighed resignedly and said, mostly to himself, "Always war. Always. It interrupts living. Our work." His words hinted at the weariness of a great musician manning a machine gun pointed at Omaha Beach—where the ocean caressed and harassed the sand, eternally and waited for blood to enrich the water and then the damp earth. Only the music of his maestro Philippe gave him a reason to look forward.

Philippe was a realist, as well, but he felt his pupil's resignation and without thinking about anything but the remoteness of hope said, "There is only one event, one only, I say, that could possibly stop the Beast of War." Hans and Ty leaned towards the maestro as he continued. "If a mighty machine, flown from a planet tens of millions of miles distant, landed in Central Park with weapons of unlimited range that could turn diamonds to dust . . . and . . . and Jesus Christ Himself was resurrected right in front of the Eiffel Tower, the guns of earth would finally stop firing."

The silence that followed was absolute.

Philippe sighed, then continued, "The intellectuals, the clever, the bright, are the easiest to brainwash. Of course, the truth is, they actually do know, but can never bring themselves to admit they have been had."

"War is like wealth. It never really vanishes, it simply changes hands," Hans contributed.

"In all of recorded history, I don't recall any happily retired dictators," Ty chimed in.

"One consolation prize, gentlemen," Phillipe added. "Everything falls in time. Gravity cinches that."

Ty raised an invisible glass for a toast. Smiling, he said, "Ah, hell, boys, drink up. There is just this world and one more anyway."

Philippe and Hans raised their imaginary glasses, clinked them, and had a hearty laugh. Ty laughed his own laugh, his alone, and couldn't stop. They formed a trio of mirth until the tears fell like rain. The cleansing slowed as Renée approached. "Oh, boys, it's wine time," Philippe announced.

Hans repeated, "Wine time."

Ty chimed in, "Time for wine time," feeling silly but not caring.

Renée had three bottles tonight. She set one aside, saying, "The Didots will join us before dinner for a toast to the safe return of their children—the children of us all." She smiled as she poured, a smile to repair bombed-out bridges and make Ty Hale's heart skip at least three beats. All he could remember was that some time, somewhere at Château Gaston, she had said, "Mother Eva wanted me to sing." Somehow he knew she would tonight. His heart resumed its regular beat.

Ty silently thought about Renée. Why did she hesitate to sing? She could have no better background or training with the musical genius of her parents and their abundantly talented associates. The war had magically swept into, through, and past the undamaged Château Gaston, leaving her father, Hans, herself, and the Didots to carry the banner. Was it Eva? The hints of something wrong, some unspoken repugnance. . . . Ty pondered, but could not ask. No one would openly, fully explain. He needed to know, if he was to remain a part of the family, as he had been made to feel over and over. Soon. Maybe.

At this moment he felt that Renée could not be improved on. Her enjoyment of the smallest and biggest events of nature, her artistic heritage, the combination of passion and gentility were beyond a young man's dreams. Today she seemed touched with a special glow. Her hair was combed out long and full, catching little lights from the sun in a reddish radiance that complimented the green of her eyes and the creamy blush of her skin. Her smile was joyful, her exuberance contagious.

After the wine was poured, the proud father stroked his gray bearded face into a broad smile, directing it toward his daughter, and passed it on to all. He raised his glass, saying, "To the sky."

Hans pushed his long fingers against his thick hair behind and said, "To the soil."

Renée didn't hesitate in moving to click all their glasses together as she pronounced, "To the world and all that's in it."

They drank to that. "Hear, hear!" Then came comforting companionship and wide-ranging conversation.

Philippe Gaston, in his elegant manner, talked a moment of Tolstoy's greatest novel and said, "The only criticism I have is the title."

The rest of the table waited.

Then he added, "I truly feel, at this instant, it would have been better to call it *War and a Few Peaceful Moments*."

Renée looked away towards the battle, still audible in the distance, then she turned her head back to the group with a smile that would melt ice and said, "The moments. The moments we should all cherish are the moments of memory. Total recall of the best."

The others made their own sounds of agreement, for the moment anyway. This moment.

"Since war is so definite, so devastating, so near," said Hans, "I would like to propose a toast to one of your countrymen, Maestro." The three looked intensely at Hans Heinke, for he spoke mostly through the piano. "To Honoré de Balzac, who said, 'The family will always be the foundation of society.'"

Everyone in the music room, the room round like the world, uttered sounds of agreement and clinked their glasses to the long past Greats.

Ty relished this talk of the old master writers of Russia and France. This was a world he knew something about, thanks to Jiggs, who had practically forced him to read the best. He had been pained at first, feeling put upon, although he was allowed to read anything he wished, as long as he did read. It was later, when he went to college, that he haunted the library to search out the masters for the thoughts and the pure pleasure he absorbed in doing so.

At dusk, the old Didots and the young prodigals came to the round house. The maestro poured from the special bottle. They all stood in a circle around the table as he toasted, "To the reuniting of our family. Blessings and thankfulness."

They sat on the porch making small talk for a while, discussing crops, cows, and the stretch of beautiful weather. After they had relaxed, Renée moved to whisper something to Hans. He arose, bowing slightly to all, and entered the round room. She whispered in her father's ear and he broke into a smile. He stood as if posing for Michelangelo and spoke, "Renée Gaston is going to sing. We must go inside to make preparations, then we will give notice to you, our audience." He made one motion with an extended arm that covered Ty and the five Didots.

There were sounds of preparation that none in the outside audience understood—the sound of the violin, the piano, and the voice of Renée, in little bursts. Those who made these sounds were loading guns for the hunt, sharpening scythes for the cutting of hay, kneading dough for baking, greasing wagon hubs preparing for a journey.

Soon Philippe came to the archway and motioned them in. Ty had some difficulty in getting the Didots to move ahead of him to the benches but finally accomplished it. The Didots sat up straight, stiff, soundless, and almost motionless. Ty joined them on the uppermost bench.

Hans ran off a few lightly touched notes as Philippe drew the bow tenderly across the violin strings. Philippe had given up much of his own classical career to play popular French songs for Eva around the world, in America, England, Germany, France, Japan, and Russia. Most audiences were amazed that a single violin in the hands of a classical master could perform so well for Eva's popular voice. When Hans joined them to form the trio, acceptance was complete.

The trio was ready and now performed for the entire audience of six, or seven, if you counted the unborn child of the Didots' daughter.

Renée's voice enveloped the round room like a mist. She started off with a medley of songs made popular by Maurice Chevalier—"Louise," "Ma Pomme," "Mimi"—starting in French and then mixing stanzas and verses in German, French, and English as Eva had taught her. The transitions from one language to another were as smooth and natural as drinking fine wine and every bit as intoxicating. The three performers blended into one sublime instrument.

The Didots sat rigid in their plain starched clothes at first and then from Nicholas's shoulder Ty could feel the beginning of swaying and physical reaction to the performance. The music banished their worries, their position, the fatigue of constant labor. Their blood and fibers relaxed and joined the hypnotic mellifluous voice and music in a totality.

Ty was equally entranced, but there was more for him. Renée was singing with her whole body, and he was so conscious of it, this supple body he thought he knew and knew he loved. Now there was more. She was generous with her soul. Now, she exuded all of it as she segued into "Mon Apéro," the song Piaf had entranced millions with.

Finally, looking at and into Corporal Ty Hale, she sprinkled the very air with the splendor of her voice, her entirety, with "You Brought a New Kind of Love to Me," which she sang in English.

It enveloped Ty's heart, lungs, his bloodstream. The ectoplasm of Renée Gaston floated with her voice into his soul.

She bowed to the seven and pointed to Philippe and Hans, who both stood up and pointed to Renée.

The Didots stood. Forgetting everything else, they yelled and clapped in abandon. Ty couldn't rise for a couple of beats. He was in a world all alone with Renée. He felt bewitched and beholden at the same blink.

Then he came back to reality and stood clapping weakly and smiling at her. He moved slowly toward her and somehow mustered the strength to ascend the two steps onto the stage. She knew. Renée folded into his arms like a Christmas gift. He held her. She held him. They parted reluctantly.

Ty hugged both Philippe and Hans and murmured, "Thank you. Thank you for the crazy world." Then he went back to Renée, who was leaning from the stage shaking the hands of the lined-up Didots. She thanked them for coming. They left the round room in single file as they had entered.

Hans closed the piano. Philippe put his violin in its case. They followed Ty and Renée back to the great room for dinner, a few wines and a brandy. Then to the portrait of Eva for the evening's final toast.

Philippe glanced at Ty and Renée with their arms around each other's waists and raised his glass. "We thank you, Eva, for passing your beauty down. You live on in grace and love, my darling."

It was an enthralling time, these last few seconds, hours, eternities. It was a difficult goodnight, though, for Renée and Ty. She had made her vow and now felt sure he was permanent, as solid and sure as steel. But she needed confirmation from him.

Ty couldn't think. All he could do was feel, and his emotions were bubbling over.

thirteen

The hearts of the French always abide in the countryside. No matter where they are, they long for it. They need it to complete their souls. Corporal Ty Hale, a man of the land himself, understood the sense of place here at Château Gaston. He had found a surprisingly fast friendship within this extended family. Such comfort! No one had questioned the soldier. For all they really knew he could be a deserter like Hans. Ty was hesitant to leave this cocoon of contentment. Even so, after Renée's unforgettable performance he was more eager than ever to know the unspoken story of Eva. What a fool he was to question anything about his haven! But he knew that these people who had given him so much were suffering deeply. He owed it to them and to himself to be part of that pain. These meandering thoughts were dangerous because he had been relieved from the terrible nausea, pain, and pondering that had caused him to have gaps in his fence-line of memory. Thinking enough to remember his recent past could demolish his present escape into almost pure joy.

He rode beside her now on one of the Arabians. She was mounted on the other. They were working these graceful, smooth-gaited animals, riding side by side circling in the huge exercise corral.

"Your father says you have your mother's voice and your own as a bonus."

"He said that?"

"Yes."

"Well, after all, fathers are usually prejudiced about their only daughters."

"True, but not the maestro. He is known to teach for skills not praise—according to Hans."

Renée, suddenly occupied with her horse, reined the gray gelding in the middle of the ring, practicing turns and stops with much expertise. Ty rode in the largest circle wondering how to approach her about the Eva mystery. He marveled at the smooth feeling of power his horse somehow gave him. It was true like all clichés: there was nothing as good for the inside of a man as the outside of a horse. He had been in the walking infantry for such a long spell that having something carry him almost gave him a feeling of guilt. Almost.

She was back beside him now, her mount still not heated up in this moderate temperature. For an Arabian a twenty-mile canter across a sun-baked desert was just barely a warm-up.

They pulled up, side by side, giving the horses a break.

Renée suddenly began to talk, "General Eubanks saved me as well as mother. His protection kept us safe from his staff and other soldiers. His family had followed papa's international performing long before he fell in love with my mother. He truly felt honored to be headquartered at Château Gaston."

"Mark one up for the enemy," said Ty sincerely.

"His orders were strict. None of us were to be abused in any fashion. I don't know why, but after he had set up his office in the library he was even more respectful."

"Who wouldn't be, with the photos of Philippe and Eva playing command performances for the royalty of the civilized world?"

"Of course. I forget about that."

"Well, you would, for you come from generations of notable people," Ty reminded her.

"Okay, but, there were a lot of sons of bitches along the way as well. Wastrels of the first and second order."

"Ah, that's just nature. You can breed the best conformed cattle for years and then one day some thin-boned, numb-skulled little bastard will just suddenly show up. It's natural, that's all. Even Mother Nature has her failings. There is no guarantee of perfection."

"You're being too kind, dear Ty," and she laughed a little, "and far too wise for your years."

"Now you're the one putting me on."

"I could feel all his staff undressing me covertly, but never where the general would suspect. It was mama Eva who entranced them most. She was in fine physical shape for her age, you know and her voice was meant to excite men of all ages and orders."

Ty started to tell Renée that nothing, no one, could touch *her* voice, but kept his lips together.

After a brief silence, Renée began to relate the painful tragedy. It came pouring from her. At first she spoke softly. As the story poured out, her voice moderated. It was so deeply imprinted in her mind that she sounded as if she were reading it aloud.

"The general entertained nightly in the great room with various officers from the fortress fronts of Utah, Omaha, and Juno Beaches. Members of the Führer's staff heard about the dinners here at the Château Gaston. They managed, while on inspection tours, to be included in the wealthy, powerful general's beneficence, which meant they could also share the talents of Philippe and Eva Gaston. After all, *she* had sung for Hitler. Even though no one in the theater was aware of Hitler's presence, she was always the lady who sang for Hitler, and that was enough to awe the listeners from the Third Reich.

"They supplied our cellars, our larders, and the kitchen itself with the finest food and wine. All of us at the château felt guilt and fear alike.

"There were almost nightly performances by Philippe and Eva. Command performances. The general's staff served the meals in the elaborate manner often adopted by those new to power and wealth. Eva sang the general's favorite songs, 'Yop La Boum' and 'Un Gars d'Menilmontant,' at least five nights a week. Month after month they played and sang to the enemy. The German soldiers clapped and shouted at the special talent before them. Odd, for with just a nod, the general could have erased them and everyone at Château Gaston forever.

"The responsibility was born bravely and without diminishing their talent. Philippe and Eva were becoming famous all over again throughout the command structure of the German army. General Eubank relished this power and the respect it provided him.

"The head of Eubanks's serving staff was named Baum. This man saw to every detail. He remembered everyone's preference in drinks especially. Because of this efficiency, he was allowed to stand back from the great entryway to the kitchen and wine cellar underneath and listen to Eva's performances. I watched him sometimes; he smiled and applauded every performance. Mother included him in her acknowledgment of the applause. She would sweep the room after bowing, with a dazzling smile. Baum began to feel her smiles were for him alone. He saw how her favored glance dwelt on him far more than the others. So, in his private elation at this secret just he and Eva shared, he drank a little more each week.

"Baum had fallen in love with one of the world's most beautiful, cultured voices. He must have believed that Eva was singing for him alone. I'm sure he thought she was glancing at others to hide her love for him. He was dead certain. Yes.

"Then it happened, the event that in one way or the other touches us all. Mother was totally exhausted from pleasing what must have seemed to her the entire German army. She had to relax alone, so she stayed up to listen to a little Beethoven on the Victrola in the library. Father and I understood and went to bed. Baum understood as well. He had drunk from the brandy bottles more than ever. It was obvious he felt something special was happening between the two of them. He had seen her move alone to the library. He swore to himself she had glanced back to signal him. At last.

"He hurried his underlings in their cleaning up. Secured an extra bottle of brandy. Shaking in anticipation of the inevitable rendezvous with the love of his life. Her love, her flesh, would be his as it was always meant to be. This was no world of coincidence. No. This was fate. Neither one had any other choice. In his mind, she had chosen him, Baum Stutz above all others. Now every dream would be fulfilled." Renée told her story as if she was reading a novel to Ty. It had become that to her.

"He entered, tiptoeing through the door to the library. Eva leaned back in the reading chair, her eyes closed, absorbed in the resounding music, relaxing her tired body and giving herself over to the greatest of classical music played by someone else. She dozed. Her head dropped almost to her breasts, awakening her. Her first thought upon seeing the grinning Baum was that she was dreaming. But Baum loomed huge and real above her. He was pouring the brandy in two glasses filling them. He spoke to her in German, knowing she understood,

"'Ah, my darling Eva, at last we are together.'

"Eva pushed herself back into the chair as if she could escape this apparition. Then she thought, '*Oh, my God. He's real.*' She could smell him. She was revolted in an instant. She hissed at him, 'Get out of here, now! Now, do you hear?'

"'Ah, my darling, it is all right to voice your love. No one can hear. You don't have to pretend any longer. We are free to express our true feelings.' Baum left the brandy on the reading table and leaned over Eva, touching her perfect coiffure, caressing her hair gently, saying ever so softly, 'At last, at last, the long wait is over. We can love freely.' He slid his hands to her neck, rubbing clumsily.

"Eva bit his wrist. He jerked back. His already heavy breathing escalated. 'Oh, so that is how you like it? What a pleasant surprise!' In a sudden move Baum ripped her dress and brassiere in front revealing her breasts. He grabbled them both, squeezing them.

"Eva raked her long fingernails across his face, searching for his eyes. She drew bloody tracks across his forehead and down one cheek. She was trying to scream and knee him in the groin, but only succeeded in revealing her long legs. Baum lost whatever control he had left. He had held back so long with patience and consideration for her position, but he could see the desire in her eyes every evening. Baum. Baum the desired.

"He hit her jaw. She was still conscious but the room was spinning around her. Her hands were reaching out for him, but they were helpless now.

"He said proudly, as if excusing his actions, 'My woman, my love, sang for Herr Hitler and she sang for me even more.' Baum dragged her from the chair. Holding her arms to the floor, he raped her. It didn't last long, but it seemed several lifetimes to Eva. Everything gathered in her throat and choked her.

"All Baum's dreams of tender love lasting endless hours had burst from him in a few greedy thrusts. He was angry about that and slapped her on the jaw again, and then again. He wanted to kill her now. She had hurried his dreams, thereby diminishing them—and him.

"She lay there, her dress pushed up above her navel, unmoving. Baum was suddenly afraid. Was she dead? With his own chest heaving so in passion and anger, he could not see if she was still breathing.

"His mind was shattered like a dropped dish. He had to get out of here and hide. Hide what? Oh, the brandy and the glasses must be moved. First, he pulled her dress back trying to cover her naked body. He stuffed her panties in his pocket and tried to pull the torn dress back over her breasts. Nothing worked properly.

"He must leave. No one had seen him. The thousands of books and the heavy door made the library almost soundproof. He took the brandy, spilling one of the glasses onto the deep rose-patterned rug. It was absorbed. He opened the heavy door to the great room. All was clear except his frazzled mind.

"He replaced the bottles in a kitchen cupboard where they were stored as always to be used the next musical evening. Then it must have come to him shockingly that there would be no more of those musical evenings. His love had succumbed to love, permanently. It was too much, far too much, for a general's orderly. He stuck an almost full bottle of brandy inside his shirt and headed for the squad tent that was camouflaged in the orchard. The guards were used to him returning there every night. They paid him no mind except to nod politely. After all, he served the general.

"He sat on his cot all night drinking brandy, except for a few stumbling trips to the latrine. Baum Stutz's mind was badly confused, and intermingled was the coldest of fear. What had he done? Nothing to feel guilty about. She had lured him with smiles, loving looks and her soft-as-cotton singing voice promised him so much. It was all her fault. She is the one who should be condemned. Eva Gaston deserved the rough but loving touch she had asked for. Drink. There is no problem. No one would ever know the two lovers had met. Drink some more.

"He didn't notice the torn silk underwear drop from his pocket to the floor of the squad tent. Drink. Empty. Sleepy. Very sleepy. Down, prone on the cot, brandy bottle drops from his hand by Eva's undergarment. Oblivion." Renée reached forward with one hand to steady herself on the horse's neck.

Ty saw that Renée was pale as skim milk. He was afraid she was going to fall from her horse. He dismounted quickly and moved to help her down. She dropped right into his arms. He put his arm around her waist, holding her steady, and took the reins of both horses. They all walked toward the stables. She tried to continue talking, but the words would not come.

fourteen

In spite of her weakened condition, Renée insisted on helping Ty brush and feed the horses before she continued her story.

Renée fell into a deep sleep after leaving her parents' performance. About an hour later, she became conscious of a tapping on her bedroom door. She listened, puzzled, her eyes forced open. Then the almost unrecognizable pleading sound of a voice awakened her more fully. It was her mother. Renée leapt from the bed and to the door, turned the lock and opened it all in one wild motion. Her mother was on hands and knees like a dog. Renée pulled her inside with adrenaline-fueled strength and lifted her up on the bed. She placed pillows behind her back and propped her up. She rushed to get water from the pitcher on her night table, and encouraged her mother to drink.

Suddenly, Eva gasped and fell into her daughter's arms sobbing. Her body shook uncontrollably, but she managed to weep almost silently.

Renée stroked her mother's tangled hair and kissed her wet cheeks as she spoke softly. "It's going to be all right, mother. I'm here. Nothing can hurt you now."

Slowly Eva's agony subsided, and in a sudden burst she told her daughter what had happened. A great rage built inside Renée. The pistol in her nightstand seemed an instant answer, but Eva, with a strength only mothers can display, ripped it from her hand. The discipline that had taken Eva out of Marseille to Paris, London, Munich, St. Petersburg, the world came into play now. Speaking forcefully, she explained to Renée that this was not the time for panic. Now was the moment for total control. Her father must be their principal concern now. He must not know of this, not yet.

Renée was almost ill. Marseille, a seaside city over 2,500 years old, was filled with cultures and pleasures. The people of Eva's home city were independent, strong willed. They had survived unscathed by rulers from Hitler all the way back to Caesar. Her family were famed chocolatiers to the best shops in Europe. To leave such a city to try and conquer the world with her voice must not end so suddenly and sordidly.

So it was decided. Eva would move down the hallway to a guest suite and Renée would explain to her father that her mother was having one of her all-alone spells. The Gastons respected the need for solitude. It was part of the rhythm of classical musicians, and of all life.

Renée grew calm. Her mother's voice had always soothed her. She put the weapon back in the drawer. They must keep their control.

The German occupiers were, in part, members of their household. The château, the owners, their servants, the neighbors, the horses, cows, geese, everything had been protected because General Eubank was in residence and because of his respect and love for the talents of the Gastons. Philippe and Eva were his relief from the greatest of all wars. Countless millions were dying violently and as many more in hidden prisons and gulags around the world. Here at Château Gaston a small pocket of beauty had been preserved. Eva repeated to Renée how blessed they were and how blessed they had been to have a gift that charmed the most powerful general. It must be maintained. Everything that they cherished could be lost forever in one careless moment.

Renée rose to the occasion. Survival was all important. It must dominate for now. She got her mother into the alone room and made her as comfortable as possible in the huge four-poster bed. She left a sleeping potion on the bedside table for Eva to take if she wanted it.

By now the sun was almost up. The two Gaston women had used all their inner and outer strength to shield the ancient chalet and all it contained.

Having calmed her mother as much as possible, Renée dressed herself, preparing to meet her father. He always got up with the sun. She waited, knowing that in a moment she would hear her father open the door, step into the hallway, and head past her door to the breakfast room downstairs near the kitchen.

They had a morning ritual. Renée would follow him downstairs. They drank coffee and visited about the farm and the livestock in the succulent green pastures. Sometimes they talked of music. Then Eva would arrive. Her presence gave a surge of limitless vitality and hope to the air itself, but not this morning in August 1944.

There was a growing babble emanating from the soldiers' encampment in the orchard. It grew louder and then still as the boots came stomping past the chalet, one soldier on each side of Baum Stutz, dragging him forward by the arms. The officers marched stiffly in the rear. The heavily muscled general exuded fury. His eyes were enraged, his ham-sized hands closed, opened, closed, opened, ready to tear Stutz into bloody pieces.

Renée could not help herself She leapt up and followed the parade, motioning her father to stay. He didn't.

The officers formed a line. In front of them the two soldiers forced Stutz to his knees. One held him by the neck bending his face down at the graveled earth that covered the entryway to the

Château Gaston. The general jerked his pistol, a P.38, out of its holster. He turned to the line of officers. "And how does this officer's court render as a verdict for one Sergeant Baum Stutz for his dastardly deed?" He already knew the answer they would give.

The officers all clicked their heels in the sharp, hard-leather sound of the German army and loudly proclaimed, "Death to the vile perpetrator."

The two soldiers stepped back. Before Stutz could move or speak, the general stepped forward, placing the snout of the gun at the back of Stutz's head, pulled the trigger and blew a piece of bone followed by a smattering of brains out of Stutz's forehead. The general stepped back. Stutz's upper body fell forward leaving him locked in a kneeling position almost like a Muslim at prayer. One of the soldiers stepped forward, raised one foot, and pushed him sideways to the ground. Then they dragged him to a military vehicle, threw him in, and hauled him away.

The general saw the pale faces of Renée and Philippe peering through the gateway. He stepped over and briskly apologized to the Gastons, finishing with "I would have been honored to soak him with gasoline and throw him into the fires of hell myself," and he held up his huge hands clenching them with much force. "Please give my deepest regrets to Eva Gaston. It is beyond me to do more for her."

As he turned back to the waiting soldiers, Renée was startled to see tears in the eyes of this man who had just executed one of his own soldiers with no feeling except outrage. His tears were for Eva.

In stunned disbelief, Philippe grabbed Renée's shoulder. "What on earth is he talking about? What is all this? Is Eva all right? Is something wrong with Eva?"

Renée took his hand, stroking it, trying to give calm and comfort to her father before she had to tell him the agonizing news.

fifteen

The two young people walked along the creek for solace as she finished relating the rape of Eva and its effect on Château Gaston and its surroundings.

"That first night after the execution of Stutz was nerveracking. The general entertained his fellow officers with ribald stories, and he showed admirable deference to father."

"I don't see how your father made dinner."

"Well, I know he was suffering terribly but he said it was what Eva would want him to do. I could tell there was no point in arguing."

"Lordy mercy," Ty said using one of his grandmother's favorite expressions without being aware of it.

"Oh, he managed to get through dinner and then even played the violin for almost an hour. I was dying inside, but my pain had to be minute compared to his. I was with mother in the alone room when she shushed me. At first I thought she was imagining something, and then I heard father's violin music coming up the stairway to us. Faint, but certain."

Ty said looking across the soothing pastures where some cream-hued cows grazed peacefully. "It's beyond me . . . how . . ., just how could any of you manage it?"

"Yes, it stunned me—but the very next evening I went to see if mother needed anything and there she stood in a long formal dress, her hair perfect, her makeup beyond reproach. 'Am I ready?' she asked. I tried to plead with her, but it was no use. She told me to think of the past and the future, then she marched out of the alone room saying, 'The show must continue until there is peace surrounding Château Gaston.' I just couldn't believe it," Renée said.

"Lordy mercy! I can't even imagine such courage."

"I couldn't either. I was so afraid for both of them, but she never sang better. She continued night after night. Each and every evening took a little of her flesh, and of course, her heart. I can't even begin to think how and what my father felt as well." She paused a moment before continuing her account. "Late one afternoon, while father was out at the barns, I went to their room as if some big magnet had drawn me. She was sitting up in bed and seemed to be expecting me. Her clothes for the evening were all laid out neatly. She had already fixed her hair, everything. She was ready for her performance, even eager. I was touched instantly by her glowing beauty and by the hollows in her face. It was a mixed feeling I'd never had before. 'I knew you would come,' she said. I pulled a chair over and sat by her, and she examined my face like a mother looking at her month-old firstborn. Then she looked into my eyes and said, 'Renée, dear, you must sing. You must.'" Renée stopped talking and walking now. She simply stood there staring at the creek.

Ty felt many things, but before he could voice any of them, Renée turned to look at him, choking back a sob. "Oh, Ty, those were the last words she ever said. All the light and life left her."

"Eva died in battle," Ty finally said.

"Yes. Yes, she did. Hold me again, Ty, as if I were the only person left in the world."

He did.

Insects made their own distinct music all around. A crow called another for its location and a calf bawled for its mother.

sixteen

The day after Eva's death, an American Infantry battalion was advancing on Château Gaston. Fighter bombers buzzed by now and then, but had orders not to damage the chalet. The Americans were eager to capture the German general and his papers, but he was just ahead of them. The Germans escaped the château with all the maps and papers intact. At the moment of their departure, the general spotted Renée and Philippe on a slight rise a hundred yards or so in front of the round room. This was the site of Eva's grave. The general stood as straight as his heavy body would allow, clicked his heels, and saluted them. They gave him a brief wave back and then the vehicles full of soldiers roared away behind the general's car.

After the German soldiers had left, the Americans swarmed the château. They found nothing belonging to the general and they took nothing but a few half-green apples from the trees and water from the creek. Soon the Americans, too, were gone, and the Château Gaston had survived again, as it had so often over the centuries.

The Didots came out of various hiding places. The cows and sheep grazed on. The crows still flew about hunting anything edible, talking all the while. Only the horses were skittish for they could hear and feel the explosions of rifle bullets, machine gun shells, and artillery in the near distance.

Ty and Renée rode over the undulating fields. Ty was surprised at how high the hills were.

Hill 192. The number crossed his mind, but he didn't know why. He forced it out of his mind. This wasn't the day for that sort of struggle.

The Arabians moved so easily that they seemed to level out the hills. The brush and trees were not so thick that they obscured the flesh of the landscape. They appeared to be growing mostly where the productive grass and edible shrubs could not. This land, of course, had been worked, fought over, and cared for so long it seemed to be permanent as the Alps.

Robins, bluebirds, sparrows, and crows flew through the trees as if teasing the two young people with their beauty and magical grace. They made all the growth of the hillsides seem more important. "What would the world be without birds?" Renée wondered.

"Less," Ty answered emphatically.

They followed an ancient trail single file now. The creek that gave life to the Gaston land had become smaller, seeking the lowest drainage course.

Then they were there. It was a marsh. The little streams that came out of the earth were hard to spot because of all the moisture. Here it was born and here it made its escape to other worlds and other creatures below as it snaked into the river far away and then to the all consuming sea. There was a rock watering-trough that had been carefully placed so as to catch pure water seepage. They rode their horses to the tank, where the animals sank their soft velvet muzzles and took long, slow swallows, relishing the sweet, new water. Ty enjoyed watering horses. They always drank with such relish, such dignity, he thought.

When the horses were sated, Renée said, "All right, you have seen the source of life! Now I must show you what results from this flow. Okay?"

The pastures above the springs were bordered by an ancient rock fence meandering over the hills. Ty and Renée rode side by side up the hill. At the crest Renée reined up. In the valley below were grain fields, houses, and a graveyard. To the right was the tiny village of Léon.

"That is the Gaston family graveyard. As you can see, it is quite large. Many, many generations of my ancestors are at rest there." Renée looked at him to gauge his interest, then smiled at the intensity of his gaze, which had swung back to the farms. "All those shelters and fields are ours," she continued. "We share them fifty-fifty with individual families. Some families have been there through six or seven generations."

Ty spoke now almost to himself but she heard clearly, "Plant the wheat in the fall. Harvest in June. Seven bundles to a stack. Threshers, straw monkeys, stacks, apple harvest in the early fall as well. Make cider to drink and sell at bigger markets."

A ripple pulsated through Renée's body, and she said with satisfaction in her voice, "I knew it. Ty, you'll make a great lord of the land."

He couldn't look at her. There had been too much exuberance in her voice, too much expectation.

"I must see the village," he said, reining past her. He wasn't ready for a commitment. He thought he had buried it all deep down, but many things were working their way towards awareness, stopping just under the surface not unlike the springs he and Renée had just visited.

seventeen

s they looked down on the village they saw that much of it was rubble. An American bomber with fighter escorts sailed across the sky, carrying enough to turn a small city into dust. An old man, a woman, and a child picked through the jumbled ruins of what was once their home. Small groups of workers were sorting out stones that could be used in rebuilding.

Ty knew he had seen this scene before, but from ground level. Pieces of the villages and their dead dived in and out of his head like wind-whipped snowflakes. He didn't even try to fit them together. He wished them away. The picture was not quite ready to reveal itself. He was not quite ready to handle it.

Now Renée, standing up in her stirrups, pointed to the right of the village along a roadway. "See there? Those dark objects, that's the general's convoy. Well, the remains of the general's convoy."

"Fighter bombers," Ty said.

"How do you know?"

"The story is all there. The turned-over vehicles, the burned circle of grass, the black areas fanning out. Tracer bullets exploded the gasoline in the vehicles, and a couple of bombs were near misses."

Renée was amazed at his reading of the scene. "I . . . I don't see how you. . . ."

"When I hunted in the prairies, I learned a lot of stuff like that. I was about this big." He spread his hands apart. "I loved it.

I learned to read the earth and everything that moved upon it. It's called 'reading sign.'"

"Does it work for you with people, this talent?"

"Sometimes. People are more devious than wild animals. They change their clothing and expressions all the time."

She thought an instant and said, "They change their smiles."

"And their voices."

"And their posture."

"And their minds."

"And their mates."

They giggled like a couple of four-year-olds before Renée became serious again. She said, "The Germans fought a delaying action here. The general's staff tried to escape it."

"It's my turn, Renée. How could you know all this?"

"Father has a Resistance radio. No one has found it. I don't even know where it's hidden."

"Well, good for him!"

She didn't tell him that the destruction in the village had been the Gastons' only loss to the invasion. Léon was on Gaston land. Ownership was never mentioned, for its shops were a convenience for all in the area.

She reined her horse around suddenly, turning away from the burned vehicles. For some reason Ty was pleased, but he couldn't understand why he didn't feel especially curious about the destruction. He was strongly repelled, for sure, and pleased at her guidance around and away from the swift battle, albeit tiny. The general and his staff were just another German casualty for Adolph.

A small flight of ducks whizzed east across the valley, headed for a pond. Their flight was linear. A squirrel ran across their path, its tail arched, and then leapt up a tree trunk, climbing swiftly, making chiding noises at them as they rode by. A robin hopped along the edge of a tiny spring, extracting worms from the soil and swallowing them whole. The robin cocked its head, observing the riders fearlessly.

When they topped out on a sudden rise the entire topography seemed different. There was a little forest in the valley climbing most of the way up a hill. Protruding grayish rocks formed small bluffs in the timber. The entire area had a sort of fairy-tale feeling. Ty practically expected the roar of some kind of monster to crack the air or a few gnomes to dance out of the woods.

His reverie was broken by the massive droning of another flight of bombers, British this time. He wished them well, but was sorry they had broken the little spell of delightful sorcery.

"See that long hill, the one with the large cluster of stones?" asked Renée.

"Yes. You can't miss it; it dominates the landscape."

She smiled in pleasure at his words. "That's our destination, our privilege." She rode ahead now, knowing exactly where the wide trail wound through the thickening timber.

Up and up they rode. The trees and shrubbery grew denser as they climbed, obscuring the view. When they reached the top, they tied the horses and walked around the little meadow. It felt good to stretch their legs after several hours in the saddle. Renée had proudly shown Ty Hale all the Gaston estate that could reasonably be seen in a day.

They walked about in a circle holding hands. For a while they didn't speak. They stopped a moment and looked back beyond where they had ridden. Ty was sure he could see the mist of the ocean—the beach where he had first landed on the bloody shores of Normandy. His mind misted like the far view.

He squeezed Renée's hand. She turned to him. With one hand he caressed her hair, almost red in the midday sun, and gave her a hug. Her body was warmer than the August sun. They separated regretfully when they heard a choking, gasping sound coming from the sky. Ty had heard this sound from fatally wounded soldiers on the ground. But where was the sound coming from now?

The disabled plane stuttered, shaking, with ribbons of smoke streaming behind. The wounded British bomber was weaving in a death drizzle. It moved erratically, its pilot desperately hoping to make it to the channel and home soil to die. It was not to be. The plane went down and vanished in the distance. The flaming smoke pushed a black hole in the sky before its sound reached Ty and Renée.

They stood a moment without speaking, then took a couple of deep breaths as she led him towards a rock shelf that sloped down like a huge chair. "Come," she invited him, "let's rest here in the shade."

Ty wondered what she meant by shade. Only one thin bush cast little particles of shadow flickering from a slight breeze across the stone shelf. They sat down, holding hands again. The cool, dry seat only made her warm softness more enticing The rock would have been a comfortable fit for a thirty-foot-tall giant. They lay back and stared into the limitless sky, still holding hands.

All sorts of things crossed their minds. She saw him riding, gray-templed, checking the fields and livestock of Gaston land, and she was singing to him and a child he held in his lap. Their child. She was suffused with an inner glow of love. Yes, love. It was not to be described or analyzed, only felt and acknowledged. Yes, he was the one. He was the one she had chosen. Her mind was churning so that the air was bruised for yards around.

Ty was thinking about the touch of a feather. He looked for the bird, but it was not there. He remained as still as his beating heart and flowing blood would allow. It came over him as slowly as a lazy turtle. It entered his body from below and spread to every fiber. He was full of something. It was music. It came from the great seat of stone. He remained motionless to try and fully grasp the meaning, the feeling, the magic. He thought he heard a thirty-yard bow drawn across the strings of a hundred-yard violin. The music must be from a collaboration by Beethoven, Brahms, Wagner, and other greats. But then the music became more than that. It could not be defined. It was the source that had fed the genius of these composers. He felt all, and oblivion, like an eternal orgasm. It was a song of stones, of the earth, of the stars, of the Great-Mystery-in-the-Sky. He could never have hummed it or thought of any verses to accompany it.

The music was ethereal and terrestrial at the same instant. It had formed in the stone as the stone had been formed. All of it and all of him had come to the earth with a falling star from an immeasurable distance so long ago as to be past human understanding. Yet in a moment he felt comfortable, relaxed, and at home, even though what he heard and felt were far beyond his understanding. He must simply accept it, like real love, and accept it he did. He was pleasured mightily.

More thoughts drifted into him with the music. Here on this earth on these stones, there was only war and music. Nothing else really counted. The touch of a feather. War and music. The endless imperishable strings that held galaxies together were played by a bow of wind countless miles long. And the force that made gravity and stone carved this ethereal music straight into the stones everywhere in the universe. His elation at this discovery was unbounded. He must share it with Renée.

He sat up abruptly. She was already sitting up, smiling into his eyes with the majesty sparkling from her eyes, greener than emeralds. "I knew it! I knew it!" she cried. "You heard the music of the mountain?"

"Music? Mountain?" he said.

"Yes! Oh yes, and more. I told my father that you are the one who would hear the music. You are one of us forever now."

"One of us!" He was one of the Gaston people and part of the Gaston land. He understood her perfectly.

Together they performed the act of love in rhythm with the music of the universe. As they lay spent afterward, Ty wandered into a half-vision where he could see infinitely far back in time. A lone person marveled at the sound of a stick striking a stone; and then two sticks together, and later sticks on hide drums for war and feasting, and then the discovery of messaging with drums. Humming and chanting led to singing to enhance the simple music. After that came strings made from the entrails of various animals for stringed instruments. The discovery of metal and the making of bronze led to the making of horns and pianos, followed eventually by great performances and emotions all around the world leading to Mozart and beyond. All of it contained in the soft stones everywhere. Everywhere.

And before all that fire mixed with water had made the stones.

eighteen

Ty entered the granary and filled a bucket with mixed grain. He had hardly shut the door when the chickens flocked to him. He pitched a half-circle swath of grain across the pen, and the fowl scattered to feed. A few encircled him clucking contentedly, knowing they would be next in line for the feast.

Ty had fed the chickens for his folks when he was a little boy. The noises of the hens and roosters had always soothed him like the best music. The chickens ate contentedly, unaware of all the hawks, foxes, and other carnivores salivating at the thought of devouring them. His grandfather used to say, "If chickens vanished from the earth overnight, there would be panic in the streets of the world the next day." When his grandmother served fried chicken and hot biscuits, they cleaned their plates without a thought of the providence of chickens around the world.

Now Ty took his time scattering the feed to the sound of appreciative clucking. He turned the bucket upside down and returned it to the granary. He looked for ol' Didot to see if he could help him with anything else. Doing familiar chores helped settle his mind.

He found Didot in the equipment yard. The old man smiled but refused his offer of help. "Thank you, Corporal, but I'm just greasing this old wagon." It was obvious that the old man enjoyed this task as much as Ty enjoyed feeding the chickens. "The maestro bought this wagon for me brand new when I was just a youngster,"

Didot said, smearing grease on the front axle with a wooden spatula as proudly as Rembrandt finishing a portrait.

Second only to feeding the chicken flock, Ty's favorite chore was milking the cows with Didot. He loved to watch them contentedly chewing their cuds. He delighted in the sound of the first stream of milk striking the bottom of the empty bucket as he pulled their teats, draining their bulging bags of the white liquid. Every experienced milker had his or her own personal rhythm. The beautiful foaming contents of his bucket would feed babies and build bones of health and strength. The cows gave, people took. Ty was thinking about all the wonderful things that came from these cows: butter on fresh vegetables and on homemade bread with jam, cream on top of strawberries. The simple act of milking in a barn full of cows, the odors of fresh hay, recalled wonderful images of his childhood.

He volunteered to help mow an irrigated pasture. The grass was used solely as hay for the horses. Didot was pleasantly surprised when Ty expertly harnessed the two-horse team and hooked them to the riding mower. Ty could drive them with a deft touch holding the reins. The six-foot mower blade was sharp, and the grass fell smoothly under the clackety-clack of its blades. As soon as this job was done, they used two teams of horses to pull the hay rakes. Didot and Ty were in sync and with almost perfect timing, they lifted the tongs, placing the hay in long windrows completely across the field. When the hay had dried, they forked it onto a wagon and stacked it in the barn alongside the stables.

Ty was almost as happy working the earth as he was looking into the emerald eyes of Renée. Almost. They both gave him a feeling of being at home. That feeling was always undercut by the thought of the portion of his mind that had recently gone missing.

Not so with Didot. He bragged proudly to his wife and looked forward to telling his neighbors, when they came back from the war, about the many surprising abilities of his friend Ty Hale. He hoped fervently for that day to come.

What did the ruling class of Château Gaston think about this breaking of tradition? Ty Hale never gave the question a thought. The work was as natural to him as breathing. Work was life.

It was a day of delight. All of them were doing things they enjoyed. Mme Didot was cleaning an already-clean room for her recently returned children. Old Didot was pampering the wagon, his favorite piece of equipment in all the world; the two maestros had just entered the Round Room to discuss genius with genius; and Corporal Ty Hale felt suddenly free to take what had become his favorite walk in all the world, a stroll along the banks of Gaston Creek. He enjoyed the walk more when Renée accompanied him, but she was comfortably ensconced in the vast library studying the praise of her mother Eva in many periodicals and books.

Before Ty went out, he suddenly broke one of his rules. He asked Didot a personal question. "I was wondering, did you hear Renée sing when she was just a child?"

Didot set the bucket down in the bed of the wagon, wiped at his hands with a clean rag, and smiled so broadly his eyes almost disappeared in the crinkles of his face. "Oh yes, that little voice could make a cock crow at midnight. All the animals would stop and listen. She could even sing smooth as new butter while cantering on a horse."

"I wish I could have heard her."

Didot suddenly became serious. "Yes. Yes, I wish so, too." Then his eyes brightened again as if a powerful battery had been switched on in his head. "But Corporal, you'll hear her forever. Won't you?"

Ty fervently hoped so, but he couldn't answer just yet. He simply placed a hand briefly on Didot's shoulder and walked on to the murmuring creek. This freshet from the bowels of the distant hills had made survival possible for the Gastons. It had also helped Ty to survive. Here he had taken his first bath after losing his memory. When he had washed away the dirt and blood in this water, he was ready to go on. But even more precious than regaining his life was the discovery of Renée, which had also happened at Gaston Creek. The creek carried the song of the stones, ever-changing in rhythm and melody. He looked as far into the hills as he could see and then back down at the sacred pool. He tried to give his thanks, and his blessing, to the sun's striped and dazzling points of light that were ever moving, disappearing and then shining again in another liquid location. He gave blessings for the Gastons, the fish, the frogs, the countless birds and animals, both domestic and wild, that survived and flourished because of the stream's ageless gift of pleasure and life itself.

He sat down on an ancient fallen stump, gray and cracked with age. He leaned back on it and sighed blissfully. The young corporal marveled at the air, so clean and pure today that he imagined it reflected the sparkles from the creek. The air seemed beatified by the great orb in the sky. He was elated to see tiny dancing rainbows, barely visible but nonetheless full of grace.

He tried to breathe all this natural beauty into himself, but it was the misty air of floating blood droplets he tasted and smelled. He was jarred back to the part of himself that was lost, the part he must search out. For a moment the taste and smell seemed to be departing. When he dared to take another deep breath, it was pure and tasted once again of beauty. The air was the air of a Lea County prairie after a spring rain. It was Hondo Canyon above Taos after the first snow. All its little lights and refreshing caresses were Renée. He loved to walk the creek with her sharing its elation. Now he felt her closeness, their intimacy, a gift of rapture.

It was so much more than he felt he deserved. A tinge of guilt at this largesse touched his heart. And even more guilt plunged knives into his soul for he knew, absolutely knew, he should be in the foxholes with his men. He stared into the blue Norman sky—even here there were moving areas of green like her eyes—and desperately wished he could stay.

He dozed awhile. Then he awakened slowly to the sound of Mozart from the Round House. Lazily he twisted his relaxed body around the stump so he could see the music. Yes, "see" it. His grandfather's influence had made him so totally aware and appreciative of music that he always *saw* it. The sounds created moving shapes. Mozart's musical notes formed three and a half spinning, transparent clouds shaped like flattened tornadoes, sometimes spinning like tops and changing to colors so vivid he could not call them blue or red or anything. They were separate from all other spectrums. They were Mozart's alone. The shapes pulsated with flashes like lightning in a faraway storm. They pulsated with both enormous pleasure and agony, all contained in the forms Mozart had given them.

Tchaikovsky's compositions bulged and undulated more sideways than upwards, abruptly changing shapes and positions and often settling to a soft mass not unlike cream in coffee. All great music was endlessly moving, changing, with indescribable coloration. Johann was Ty's favorite of the Strauss family of composers. His work was horizontal. It came sailing out like the waves on a large lake taking on a fleeting life and size of their own. The waves curled upward, forming thick, inverted fishhooks, scouting the shoreline in their one moment of existence, dancing all in rhythm, to the musical genius of Johann Strauss. Billions of little multicolored lights flickered throughout the pulsating form. There were blues like miniature skies and yellow-orange like the flares of the sun. Others blinked and teased, creating cascades of crushed jewels. The movements of the shapes and colors always left Ty feeling both purified and humbled.

Beethoven was another matter entirely. Ty saw him as the inside of a single cell magnified a million or so times. A single tiny cell deep in a rocky cavern contained a world so vast that only the music gave comprehension for now. Therein was a huge world of music. Circular. Violins being played by countless bows, a horn section of shapes he had never imagined. All was movement. There were no breaks. There were whirling wheels of all sizes and relative dimensions. The main wheel was a perfect hexagon. It conducted and powered all the instruments and sounds. The wheel was the orchestra of all life. The sounds of such faraway creation and creativity were too much for Ty, but he absorbed its beauty into parts of himself he never dreamed existed.

And sometimes, ever since he had started seeing the sounds, the cells, he thought that music was the beginning of all and war would be the end of all. And then he would decide there could be no all, and he gave thanks to Beethoven and the Great-Mystery-in-the-Sky for the eternally working parts.

Knowing he was a musical dunce, he never had mentioned these visions to anyone. Maybe everyone saw the substance of music in the air, in which case it would be extremely embarrassing to bring it up.

He dozed pleasantly, and when he came back awake, his first sight was the first star of the enveloping dusk. He could see it clearly and wondered if it could see him. Of course it could, but why bother with a speck on a speck in such a vast universe.

The quiet from the round room had jarred him awake. It was wine time. He must not be late; Renée might already be there. Adrenaline jolted him into motion and he was soon running across the grassy rolling hills of Gaston country. The grass seemed softer than velvet and he never noticed the jarring of the earth that nourished it. He had always been lucky that way.

One thought stuck in his head for a second, for no reason he could fathom. Everything was relative. Everything. Before he could pursue that, he spotted Renée. She was bringing the wine and pastry tonight. Ah, blessed again. What a day for Corporal Tyson Hale of Lea County, New Mexico, and now of the great Gaston country! And there was Renée and the night left to experience. At the sight of his love, he started laughing, and as ridiculous as it seemed to him he attempted to run so fast his feet were above the earth, but they touched every now and then. Both of them.

It had been another great night at chez Gaston. Ty and Renée held hands as he walked her along the veranda to her room. He let go of her hand and turned back before they reached her doorway. He stopped in front of his room and leaned against the stone railing. Staring as hard as he could into the star-blinking sky, he realized again that the event that had brought him to this moment was not visible anywhere in all that space. It was hidden somewhere inside him. In his skull. His brain. His memory. Part of the last was missing. The pain of searching for it distressed him, but this was no moment for pain.

Softly he spoke. "Oh, Great Mystery, I wish to thank you for allowing me to see the precious air, the beautiful sky and hear the music of the water plunging out of the singing stones. My eternal gratefulness for all the people of the Gaston domain, the provocative conversations, and the grapes to make such fine wines. Hey, Great Mystery, I owe you something special for Renée. Just tell me what you want and I'll give all I have to accomplish it."

Ty hesitated a moment before he spoke again. "Please do not think I'm asking You to solve this for me . . . I only ask that you help me gather my courage and whatever knowledge is left in me to solve the puzzle of my puzzlement. I ask this humbly knowing you have endless and more important things to do. But . . . I, too, need to reach some decisions. If you have just a moment to spare. . . ."

He waited, still staring, hoping. His eyes tired as he stood at attention and briskly saluted the universe. Then he entered his room, undressed, and fell on the bed in a peaceful sleep without remembering his dreams.

nineteen

The young couple walked in a kind of reverie across the green hills with their scattered stands of trees. They held hands comfortably, silently, each with their private thoughts and feelings. They were together, that's all that mattered to them at the moment, just like all young lovers before them. Renée was smiling. Her whole being was smiling. And why not? The man she loved was a perfect fit for Château Gaston, the perfect father for a Gaston heir. She was certain of this. He understood livestock and its care. He knew the bounty of the earth firsthand. He loved books, music, and the freedom of conversation at wine time. Philippe had taken to him instantly, as had the Didots. Even the chickens he enjoyed feeding seemed happier when he was around. She was not unlike the chickens, she mused, smiling even more radiantly at this thought.

She and Ty didn't dare to look at one another because they realized that before they knew it they would be rolling in the grass. So Ty controlled himself and thought silently about other things. He knew he must solve the several mysteries that had been bothering him. Most of the time he was lost in a lovely haze of fulfillment. So much had happened. Things had always happened around him. He had found out on Music Mountain that Renée had accepted him into her world as its new keeper. Could it work? He was confident that in a short time he would understand the rhythm of Château Gaston and its rich earth. And Renée? How could he ever expect to find a woman like Renée anywhere but here? When he had everything working and profitable they could have two or three children to carry on the long traditions of this gifted land. He would teach them to ride, hunt, fish, read, and he knew the music would assert itself. Château Gaston *was* music. The greatest and rarest kind. For a moment he felt as he had on Music Mountains that the stones of the land were where music began on earth.

This place was special because it was. It was special to Ty and Renée because they had shared in the discoveries of love and mystery. Ty felt so alive, so profoundly blessed here. As he silently expressed his gratitude to the green earth and the blue sky around it all, it started to come back to him.

The beauty and peace that had consumed him rang a bell. Was he starting to remember what had happened to him before the assault on Hill 192 at Saint-Lô?

Suddenly his head was full of images. How many airplanes did it take at 30,000 feet to circle and vanish out of sight on both the east and west horizons? Why did his thoughts always go back to the sky of war? There was so much noise from the billions of tons of steel and wheeled machines moving lead, powder, food, medicine, shells, cigarettes, and even hard chocolate bars. There were the screams of the wounded and their last efforts to hold life for another breath, then another. There were the smells of blood and fire intermingled with the noise of war in all its agony, the gloating of the Beast. The warplanes still dominated, but he couldn't fit two or three jagged pieces of his puzzle in their proper spots. Maybe he hadn't put enough thought into his problem. His time at the Château had been so pleasant that he just accepted and enjoyed everyone and everything as natural. Now, though, he was beginning to realize there had been a matrix of mixed events that would fill a lifetime. He smiled as he thought back a week, two, three. A year? Always? It would be so easy to fulfill Renée's dreams for him, for them.

What would it matter if he was found out later? He would already have enjoyed life more than any human deserved. But what was there to find out exactly? No. He must not let his mind travel there now. He must keep on enjoying the present.

Suddenly he stopped and, taking her other hand, pulled her toward him. His smile filled Renée with anticipation. Her emerald-tinged eyes were looking full into his. Her face said, "What now?"

Ty looked at her a moment in appreciation beyond the words he wanted speak to her. At last, they came without thought.

"Renée, do you know what you are?"

Her face asked, "What? What am I? Are you going to tell me?"

"You, my darling," he said, "are a Strauss waltz." And he gathered her in his arms and danced her over the yielding grass of Gaston hills. They whirled and whirled and laughed and laughed and both could hear Strauss's magic music following them obediently.

A crow flew a hundred yards above them heading for a place behind the turmoil of the ground wars. The two figures swirling small below him held no interest for him . . . today.

twenty

Renée was busy seeing to the household chores and over-seeing the work of the younger Didots. Nicolas had been relieved and thrilled when his brother and two nephews returned safely to the estate. He really needed the extra help. Now he could start planning for the future of the livestock, the vegetable gardens, the orchards, and the entire grounds. He could organize for life itself and beyond.

Philippe and Hans worked with renewed dedication, arranging, perfecting, and performing their music.

As Ty walked slowly along the creek, he could hear chords from the round room. He sat a while by the water. The music of the stream made him laugh aloud with joy. Heard only by various birds and insects, a squirrel, a pair of rabbits and a small flock of fat sheep grazing nearby, his laughter subsided, leaving him even happier than he had been before. A dove plunged across the sky. Ty briefly envied its piercing flight, seemingly so swift to make up for its slightly deviant sky path. At least it knew where it was going.

Suddenly he had an irresistible urge to run. He raced along the creek feeling his pumping heart filling his lungs and propelling him forward joyfully. Patches of his childhood floated by. He caught a glimpse of the Sangre de Cristo Mountains northwest of Las Vegas, New Mexico. Some had snow-streaked tops. There were flashes of Highlands University, the track field, the huge trees on the Las Vegas plaza where General Kearny had stood atop a building and with only his voice taken the territory of New Mexico for the United States. His army hadn't fired a shot.

Then he had glimpses of his best friend, Emilio Cortez. They were laughing. Who was that? Oh, it was Emilio's sister, Elena, and she cast her head sideways as she smiled at him. Her blue eyes faded into the sparkle of the New Mexico sky, lost. They came again as she walked towards him, sinuous, sensual, inviting. Then she turned like a runway model and walked slowly into an adobe wall and became part of it. How had he missed her signals, her light? Maybe he hadn't after all.

Ty ran on and then he crossed the bridge and in a couple of beats, stopped and looked back at the house and corrals where he had been touched by a feather. He saw blue eyes vanishing into the outbuildings. They were Emilio's, his best friend for three years at the university, his best friend ever. Now his inner eyes looked into the questioning blue eyes as the round hole appeared just above the bridge of Emilio's nose. The eyes turned to unpolished chert, a very dead mineral. Everything behind them and below them became inert. Now the pattern of flesh, steel, blood, and foxholes started to come together. He saw the slow, slow movement of the bombers and fighter escorts moving like a rising moon, undetectable but certain.

It all vanished. He stood by the pool where he had seen the vision of Elena nude, walking towards him in a flawless female movement on the pool's surface without creating a single ripple.

Then there was Renée. Real. She dried her body in every spot he now knew so well. It was almost enough to make him race back to the great stone house for her. However, something else fleeting and forbidding entered his being. He needed to think carefully now. Very carefully. But the strain of seeking what he had experienced before the Gastons found him, or he found them, was interfering with his search.

The wonder of his running was leaving him. He thought of his grandparents, of Mama Jo's pride in her farm-raised meals, not unlike the Gastons.' He saw his grandfather peering at him, leading him mentally into music and classic novels. How could this be? He had gained much insight from the readings but even more pleasure. That could be understood, but the music? He was inept, for sure, when it came to playing any musical instrument. He didn't know one note from another. How could he love it so much? How did it seep into his veins, his bone marrow, his genes? How could he feel so deeply when he knew so little? Suddenly he understood that he must not question, just accept. His grandfather had always understood. Maybe he should speak with him of other things. Well, he couldn't; his grandfather's voice was on a one-way line.

"Papa J, write me a mind-letter. Mail it right now. Your grandson is in dire need."

"I'm here, Ty. I've news for you from home. We've had to form an official poker club. Too many outsiders were dropping by for free beer, and the game itself was becoming unimportant. Much as I regret this regimentation, we have some order back now. The dedication to the skills of the game, the camaraderie, the betting, the bluffing, the reading of faces and gestures has made it a game again. How's ol' Jagger, you wonder? I asked his wife, Sue, that same question at the market the other day.

"'How's ol' Jagger?' she repeated, thinking carefully before she answered, 'Oh, he goes right off.'

"'Goes right off?'

"'Yeah, right off the bluff. Right off to sleep. Right off to the hay meadow. Right off to the poker game.'

"'I stopped her before she was exhausted by saying, Well, Sue, I assume ol' Jagger is right off. Huh?'

"'You got it,' she said, picking up a head of cabbage and placing it carefully in the cart adding, 'ol' Jagger gets off on cabbage.'"

Then the grandfather laughed, as crazy as his grandson, although Ty didn't quite get as much humor out of this story as his elder did.

"Now, on the other hand, when I asked ol' Jagger about the welfare of his spouse, Sue, he said without even taking his eyes off his cards, 'She is like Listerine mouthwash, I hate to use it, but it's necessary.' Don't you see?, Ty? Everything has to fit the viewpoint."

Ty, not remembering the one-way line, asked, "And what do you mean by that?"

Grandfather went on, "You see, son, ol' Jagger has got way more years on him than me. There ain't many old-timers left. There never were many of them."

Ty could hear his grandfather's staticky chuckling. At last he came clearly back on the ectoplasmic line again.

"We have a new member in the poker club now. When that man walks through the door you've got a room full even if he's by himself. We fought in the First World War together—against one another. It binds us, as I'm sure you've found out in your own war, the next one after mine. Of course; that's silly of me. There's always a next one. Anyway, this man Beiber and I always have a lot to talk about together. The most difficult task for a man is chasing a woman or vice versa, but it always seems easy at first.

Herr Beiber said this to me, 'A female rain is gentle, caressing, clinging, persistent. A male rain is the exact opposite, but a good one is persistent.' Well, now, Ty, that's not all he said to me, there's more such as 'Souls are smarter than brains. The mother soul gives birth to original literary and musical souls just like a garden gives sustenance to a new species of tomatoes or melons.' Now, ain't my new friend Herr Beiber quite a thinker?"

Ty said, "More than I can handle properly, Papa J," but of course, his words couldn't reach the old man.

Papa J had left the line and Ty felt lonely for a moment. "Tell me just one more story, Papa J, please. Not a bedtime story, but an all-time story."

"I'll send you one more? Okay. Then off with you. Back to your foxhole, Ty. Well, as you demand. This is The Central Puzzle. Here goes. A past is proven by artifacts and scientific dating. There may be a future, but we only become cognizant of it when it has already become the past. There can never be a 'present' because everything is moving, always moving." The voice faded away.

How could he feel so cleansed, Ty wondered, when he could fathom so little of his elder's meaning? "He expects me to absorb his words before I try to analyze them," Ty said aloud to himself. "It is a compliment, even if I don't deserve it."

Ty ran toward the round room. As he ran, the music became louder and clearer. He put all the notes in his invisible music box to hold and treasure over and over again.

It felt good to run again, and he didn't stop until he was in front of the porch where he had first stopped several lifetimes ago. He sat quietly down at the table so as not to disturb the performers inside. He looked up at Eva's grave on the hill and raised an imaginary glass to her. "To you, Eva, a brave talented, and lovely woman."

He felt so at home at the large round table. He couldn't believe even now how blessed he had been to be so swiftly accepted. It was as if he sat with several grandfathers. The Gastons and their best friend, Hans Heineke, had catapulted him into places only his grandfather was familiar with, maybe even farther.

The music inside the house had stopped, but it was a few moments before Philippe and Hans joined him on the porch. It took them a few minutes to come down to his level.

At last, Philippe said, "Renée tells me you had a great ride, Ty."

"Oh, it was that and more."

Phillipe ran his fingers across his neatly trimmed mustache and beard. his eyes spoke volumes, though all he said was, "That is good to hear. My congratulations." They had all dropped the "corporal" in front of his name, and even he had stopped thinking of himself that way.

A crow landed in a lone tree near them. The bird cocked its head to see if they were having snacks it could pick at later. A distance away another crow cawed three times. The near one didn't answer, but flew off, no doubt under orders or its own kind of curiosity.

As though he were reading Ty's thoughts, Philippe commented, "Eva and I traveled the world, and I can't think of a single part of it where we weren't spoken to by crows."

Hans nodded his head.

"When I was a little kid," Ty said, "I remember them following my father's planter scratching up the single seeds almost as fast as they were put in the ground."

"They survive every way there is," Hans said. "If there was nothing for them to eat but roadkill, they would still have shiny feathers."

"They will out-survive everything but the cockroach, I do believe," Philippe added.

Ty had a laughing spell brewing, but he choked it short to say, "Aw, I think they'll learn to devour even those."

There was no telling where this idle chatter would have led, but they saw Renée coming with the wine bottle, glasses, and a plate of hors d'oeuvres prepared by Marie Didot. It pleased Ty to hear the mellifluous cheer with which Philippe sang out, "Wine-time!" It was as if they were being presented royal awards of honor.

Renée moved through the Normandy air as if she had wings. Her soft yet powerful presence made the three men sit up straighter. There was something about the way she poured the golden liquid into their glasses that gave extra light to the evening.

Today the conversation was casual. Philippe asked about Ty's homeland. "What is it about the New Mexico prairie that you find most unforgettable, Ty?"

Ty answered instantly, "The wildlife." They looked surprised. "When strangers drive through, they usually say something like, 'How could anyone live in this God-forsaken place? It is so lonely it gives me the shivers.' Or, 'There's nothing here but empty space.' But it was a great place to be a boy. When I was a small child hunting and roaming, I found the prairies full of adventures.

"There are game birds: quail, grouse, prairie chickens, and doves. Even in great droughts, jackrabbits and cottontails are everywhere. You can see beautiful meadowlarks, robins, sparrows, scissortails, butcher birds, wild canaries, and even bluebirds, some-times." Ty was getting excited. "There are great rats' nests built at the base of large mesquite bushes from their twigs, weeds, and cow chips. The rats provide sustenance for all kinds of hawks that nest in the mesquites, or any lonely tree they can find. There are snakes who hunt mice and everything small that lives on the ground. You find numerous insects, some very beautiful, as you do in most of the world. There are badgers, ground squirrels, and ground owls. On and on. Life is literally exploding, but unseen by most. I loved it all."

Hans asked, "But what about water? Does a river run through it?"

"Surface water is pretty scarce in Lea County, but great basins of water are just below the ground. There are windmills scattered around that fill tanks and ponds so all the creatures can drink, and sometimes even ducks swim in them. Of course, there are cattle by the thousands, and horses, and coyotes, and crows, of course. The coyotes take care of any surplus and the crows clean everything up, the same as they do over the rest of the world.

"There are people—real working cowboys, ranchers, farmers, oil field hands, merchants, all making their way there. Probably they are a little better at surviving than average because of the harshness of the land. The great droughts, the prairie fires, and the drastic changes in seasonal temperatures toughen them." Ty finished his speech and was suddenly embarrassed by his long-windedness. He felt he had rambled on about something his friends had no way of understanding. "I'm sorry, I just got carried away."

Seeing his discomfort, Renée came to the rescue. "It sounds so fascinating, so different from anything we know. I hope I get to experience it someday."

"I've read that there were once thousands of buffalo across all that land," Philippe remarked.

"Yes. The Indians pursued them, and we still find arrowheads and spear points where they hunted. Entire prairie tribes survived alongside the buffalo."

Renée stood to pour more wine. Ty had almost started a discourse on the slaughter of the great humped animals, but the Normandy sun sliced under the porch ceiling, surrounding Renée's head in a halo of light. He knew that vermilion glow came from her own inner sun as well as from the one sinking in the west.

Philippe proudly observed the grace and beauty of his only child. "We are very fortunate, gentlemen. Renée is going to sing for us tonight after dinner."

The anticipatory smiles on all their faces were banished by the roar of engines. A line of vehicles was powering down the road at the front of the main house. There were three command cars, a truck full of troops, and several jeeps for the lower-ranking officers.

As the first command car braked hard and doors were pushed open, Philippe said, "Go, go, go, you both know where."

Ty and Hans had been well-trained ground soldiers. They were already moving, running low and as hard as they possibly could, ducking behind the round room seeking the land just beyond the hill.

Philippe spoke abruptly to Renée. "Come, let's go to meet our company." They, too, walked fast, trying to keep the eyes of the Americans on them instead of pursuing Ty and Hans, but Colonel Klein, the commanding officer, had seen the two run. There was no reason for flight from the OSS unless one was guilty of something. He instantly ordered a squad of men to follow the fugitives. Armed with .45 caliber submachine guns and automatic side arms, the troops raced across the hills, trying to cut off Ty and Hans, who had the advantage of adrenaline as well as being heavily armed. Both feared being captured as deserters. Ty, of course, was a born runner, but Hans, a born musical genius, couldn't keep up. Ty turned back to his faltering companion to offer encouragement.

Hans was gasping for breath. His lungs had softened since his escape from the cliff above Omaha Beach, and lack of exercise had weakened him. He couldn't keep up with Ty. Desperate though he was, his legs kept buckling beneath him. Ty, of course, was in the best shape of his life, ready to run for his life. He had continued every activity the Gaston estate provided, working the pens, the fields, riding horses, and making love with Renée. He was in top shape to perform this sprint for their lives.

The cries came, "Halt. Halt. Halt, or we'll shoot!" The two escapees could hear the bullets cracking the sound barrier over their heads and ricocheting off the dirt and stones of the hills, but the distance was too great for the .45 caliber rounds to be accurate. The troops were gaining fast.

With the strength of desperation, Ty heaved Hans over his shoulder and kept running. He could feel his heart struggling to pound through his ribs and burst apart, but he kept going. Everything was gray, with flashes of red and black. Ty felt his legs wobble. Hans was slipping off his shoulder.

There were men yelling, firing bursts. Some of the rounds were very close. One clipped a rock on the hill, and it hit Ty on the cheek where the swift flying bird had touched him. The touch of a feather.

There was the sinkhole. He leapt at a steep angle to fall into the thick brush. He rolled over twice, and Hans was gone, lying flat on the slope behind him. There was no use speaking. It was too dangerous anyway. Ty turned around and grabbed Hans's arms and heaved him up on one shoulder again. The voices were just around the corner. Using Hans's buttocks to break through the shrubbery, he shoved them both through very dense brush.

They were hung up. Ty couldn't move. Then the sounds of the pursuers just beyond the crest of the sinkhole gave him a miraculous burst of strength, and they moved through the tangled growth and into a stone-masoned tunnel of darkness. Nothing mattered now but finding safety underground.

Inside the sanctuary, Ty remembered, there were niches every few feet with oil lamps and cans of matches. He felt for one and found it. He lit the lamp. The flame warmed him. He felt that he was coming back to life.

He went back and found a stunned and hapless Hans sitting up. Ty knelt down and looked him over. His friend was simply exhausted, but he was trying to thank Ty for saving his life. They couldn't risk the noise. Ty shushed Hans with a finger over his lips.

They could hear babbling voices outside. Then they faded away.

twenty-one

Philippe recognized the officer's rank. "Can we help you, Colonel?" he asked.

"Klein. Colonel Klein."

"Philippe Gaston, Colonel. My daughter, Renée."

"Who were those men who ran?" The colonel asked in French.

"Oh, those? They said they were members of the French Underground," Philippe replied offhandedly. "We invited them to have a glass of wine and rest a while. We don't ask too many questions. Many members of our family are fighting in the Underground."

"I know that, sir. But why did they run, then?"

Philippe interrupted him in English. "You speak excellent French, Colonel."

"Thank you, Sir, but that was better English than my French. Shall we proceed in English? Back to the escapists. Please, sir, I insist you identify them."

"We have to the best of our ability."

"Their names, then. Surely they introduced themselves to such loyal Frenchmen as the Gastons."

Renée took a step forward and said, "One was called Marcel, I think."

"It seems the other mentioned Pierre," said Philippe.

"That seems convenient, since both names are distinctly French." The colonel was clearly annoyed.

"We had just met. Their sudden appearance was a great surprise," Philippe insisted.

"We are on the same side, Monsieur Gaston."

"Yes, of course. That was my feeling about the two strangers. I wish we could help you more."

"One would assume members of the Underground would gladly come to meet us instead of fleeing like traitors."

Philippe and Renée were both straining for an answer. They were saved by the sound of submachine-gun fire.

"It doesn't matter now," the colonel said. "Sergeant Avolio and his squad will soon return with their bodies."

Then the barking of the guns came again. Blended voices fading away. Voices of angry desperation. Renée and Philippe quivered inside.

Colonel Klein spoke again, now in a softer voice. "It seems to me," he said to Philippe, "that it is a bit unnatural for you to work so diligently for the resistance and not be proud to introduce us to other members."

"I would be more than happy to do so if they were present, Colonel. And as I said before, they had barely arrived."

"I hope that would be the case. However, you must know, Sir, that if it is otherwise it could cause a great inconvenience for all."

Renée could contain herself no longer. "My father and countless centuries of Gastons have fought and died for France."

"Of course, of course, but this is a different war than any before. People, entire countries change sides in the blink of an eye."

"If I didn't know you were simply doing your duty, I would deeply resent that implication, Colonel," Philippe said, his face reddening.

"I am relieved that you understand, sir. Anyway, our troops will soon return with the suspects. Then we shall be free of any possible misunderstanding."

Philippe and his daughter clamped their jaws tightly, fighting their rising fear for the safety of Ty and Hans.

The colonel cleared his throat and took out a pack of cigarettes offering a smoke to Philippe and Renée, who simply shook their heads for fear their voices would give away their nervousness.

The colonel casually inhaled and slowly let the smoke exit his mouth. He spoke with careful politeness. "Of course. The fact that Eva Gaston was a great diva . . . who . . . sang for. . . ."

"My mother never sang for that . . . that beast." Renée could hold it back no longer. "I insist, Sir, that you do not call her a diva. She always insisted she sang only because she had too."

"I didn't mean. . . ."

Philippe interrupted him. "I suppose it is unavoidable that you search the premises for the inevitable report?" He put his hand on Renée's back and patted just once.

The OSS Command had set up large tents, one for the officers, one for the enlisted men. They were very thorough in their search of the Gaston estate for any intelligence General Eubank may have left behind. It was all done efficiently with the apologies of Colonel Klein. Tall and bony, he moved with smooth confidence. His face was sharp with an aquiline nose and high cheekbones that seemed to want out of his face. His eyes were dark and bright. He had somehow been born for this duty, and his men all reacted to his orders with efficiency and respect.

The soldiers missed little in their search, even opening over a thousand books in the library and riffling through them. They sounded the walls for hollow places and checked every piece of furniture for secret compartments. The colonel was heard to say, "Inch by inch, men."

The Didots were not immune. Their homes were relent-
lessly gone over, and they were grilled even harder than Philippe
and Renée. None broke. To hold out was a time-honored tradition. This was relatively easy. In the past there had been times
of torture, even of death. But they were on the same side here,
and all the Gaston estate knew that Ty and Hans had escaped.
There was, of course, a deep fear that one or both might have
been wounded, but Philippe managed to assure everyone that
there was no cause for alarm. The pursuers would have found
spots of blood and been bound to report it. This gave everyone
new hope and reinforced their polite resistance.

Ty and Hans had everything they needed to sustain them until
they were notified that it was safe to come out. Of course, Renée
was troubled by the nagging fear that they would lose patience and
be tempted to take a peek to see if the OSS was gone.

"That would be disastrous," she said to Philippe, her voice
carefully calm. "Father, we have some detailed planning and thinking to do. Our men can no longer risk being found out. We must
figure a way to make these people abandon their search."

"Yes, dear Renée. Do not worry now. There will be plenty of
time to solve our predicament." His resonant confidence allayed
her anxiety for the time being, but it soon returned. Would Ty stay?
She had planned their love as if it were a dinner menu. She and Ty
had simply accepted that they would be here forever, producing
children, crops, cattle, horses, and an abundance of all things in
a future so distant it didn't matter. The sound of gunshots aimed
at her beloved had startled her into a sudden awareness of the
uncertainty of their lives. A nausea of the soul possessed her. The
ineluctable pain that moved about under her breasts made breathing difficult. She was almost too terrified to breathe. She heard her
father's voice as if it came from a deep cavern, "Renée, don't you
hear me? Come, dear, the colonel has ordered us to the chapel."

"The chapel?" she whispered, "Oh, my God, they've found it!"

"No, no. They haven't even entered the chapel yet."

She followed him down the stone walk, its stones worn smooth by countless processions to worship, weddings, and funerals.

"Monsieur Gaston. Mademoiselle," the colonel said with polished politeness. "Out of respect for your place of worship and this esteemed family, we wish you present as we make our final search."

There was both relief and terror in the last statement. It was good to know the search was almost finished, and it was frightening to realize the men were so near the entrance to the underground chambers.

Philippe and Renée sat in the back and watched in agony as the colonel restated his instruction: "Inch by inch, men." Philippe placed his hand over Renée's and whispered, "It has not been found since . . . well, ever."

She gave him a quick smile and then froze. Eternities were whizzing by. She squeezed her father's hand until he feared she would faint.

Now an officer was at the pew that revealed the entrance to the sanctuary. Examining up, down, pushing, and thumping about. Suddenly Renée unbuttoned the top two buttons of her blouse, got up, and strode swiftly to the altar, where the silver Christ hung from a silver chain. She knelt and bent over so that a portion of her breasts was revealed, and somehow prayed.

Renée had seen one lieutenant in particular staring at her almost all the time he had been here. All women know this stare. She felt it now, the ancient stare, burning away the pain under her breasts as she prayed for the safety of Ty and Hans. The lieutenant was still inspecting the area around the altar. He breathed hard, but he knew full well that this look at her cleavage was as close as he would ever come to this beautiful creature. He knew the wish for the unattainable had downed more men than all the machine gun fire in history.

The other soldiers had already exited, and with a sigh of longing the lieutenant stepped down and walked to the doorway of the church where his commander waited. He spoke softly, "Nothing, Sir. There is nothing untoward at the Gaston estate except the mystery of the two fleeing men."

"It will have to remain so, Lieutenant. We have other far more pressing duties. I will make our apologies to the Gastons."

"That's the right thing to do, Sir."

"Yes. Yes, they are a noble family, indeed."

Inside, Philippe knelt beside his daughter. He felt that he should offer her his thanks, but under the circumstances he didn't know how.

Renée's blouse was buttoned by the time she stood up from under the silver Christ.

twenty-two

Ty felt for the lamp in the niche in the tunnel wall and lit it. While Hans was trying to pull himself together, Ty tried to straighten Hans's hair. It was sticking out in an erratic halo around the back of his head as if he had just come out of a musical spasm after composing a dozen masterpieces.

Carrying the lamp, Ty made his way to the room that held their uniforms. He checked the rifle and the .45 to make sure they were ready and placed them by the entryway to the main passage for easy access.

Ty stretched out on a cot and lay back with his eyes closed. He was communicating with his grandfather, or so he hoped. "Papa J, you must send me a mind-letter. I'm in dire need. I know that's a cliché, but like all clichés, it's true. This wish is, sure as all hell, true. You're probably ticked off because you haven't received any of my mind-letters lately. Well, you will, probably all at once. Remember when I was overseas climbing those almost vertical two-thousand-foot Welsh mountains at night to get toughened up for Normandy? I'm sure you do. Well, I got all your handwritten letters at one mail call, six months after our division moved into Wales from Ireland. That's how you'll get my letters, both written and mind mail, all at once.

"I don't know how to tell you this, but I've been on sort of a recess here in Normandy that's turned out to be both fun and educational, with some of the most sophisticated people I could ever dream up. With all their training and natural talent, I've not found any snobbery from any of them. Dammit, Papa J, I hope you make some sense out of my amateurish description of this little group. I'll go into more detail later.

"Anyway, I was enjoying my peaceful and enlightening moments so much that I forgot you once telling me, 'Smile while the sun shines, son, because the dark clouds always come back. You'll appreciate when they're gone.' Remember? Well, maybe not, because you actually worded it better than that. Forgive me.

"We had a little interruption in our idyll an hour or so ago. So you see, that's when I realized I might possibly have the time to mentally correspond with you. I try not to miss you and Mama Jo, but when I'm idle, like now, I ache to see you both and walk across the flat country again. I would even relish you loaning me and that old sorrel horse out to cowboy at roundups and brandings, yeah, and even fence building. But I'd never make it permanent because all you're gonna wind up with is your love for the job. There's no way to explain this prairie craving. My little . . . furlough has been in rolling hills, deeply grassed, well watered with springs and little creeks as well as timber of all kinds on the highest hills. It is, to an infantry soldier, a sort of paradise since he's not being shot at. Yet, I am suddenly, right now, in pain to see you both and our endless pancake prairies. I feel I must rest my head a few moments before I continue this mind-letter. I also suddenly feel well. Please excuse me for a few moments. I'll be back soon because I must seek your sage advice. Oh, hellfire. I hear Hans calling me from a great distance. No. He's right here. Stay put, I'll be right back."

"Corporal, wake up. Dinner has been served."

Ty stumbled to his feet, struggling to move back from the prairies of Lea County, New Mexico, to the Romanesque underground of Normandy. "Dinner, you say?"

"Yes. It is served. Come."

Ty followed Hans into another room built for both cooking and eating. It had hidden wiring from an outside generator. Hans had some sort of beef stew hot and ready to eat. It was made from dried beef as well as peas and other vegetables that had been preserved for such emergencies.

Smiling, his eyes twinkling through his spectacles, Hans poured a glass of 1787 Château Lafite Rothschild, a near-priceless wine. He sat down and raised his glass to Ty. "For saving my life!"

Ty was embarrassed and took a deep swallow of the smooth red liquid before he could answer, "It was nothing. I was saving myself. Don't mention it again."

Hans looked at him a moment, then motioned to the nearest wall. Leaning there were a Rembrandt, a Renoir, and a Monet.

"My God! Are those originals?"

"Of course. I would never demean this special dinner with fakes."

"But where did they come from?"

"There's an entire hidden room full of masterpieces that once hung in the Gaston Château. Goering would have requisitioned them if they had not been well hidden."

"Forgive me, Hans, I forgot how much time you've spent here."

"Ah yes, but it is far better that the alternative, don't you think?"

"Indeed. This stew is delicious, Hans. In fact, you might say this is just about the very best stew ever made."

"This is because you are very hungry."

"No, this stew has magic, like when you play Mozart on the piano."

The food was finished; more wine was poured. They discussed many things, but not their immediate problems. Suddenly

Hans's face revealed a deep emotional disturbance. Ty had to say something. He went to the center of the target with one shot.

"What are we going to do about all these problems, especially your deserting Hitler's army, friend Hans? There's got to be a solution to help us both. But so far, I just can't come up with anything."

"Believe me, Corporal, I have given it endless thought. I could not kill for a Hitler or his insane ideology, but if I didn't I would have been killed myself. Most certainly."

"It is a dilemma, *mi amigo*." The words from New Mexico fit in naturally with the French they were speaking, French being the language they could both speak with the same lack of skill.

Hans said almost reluctantly, "But you are perhaps haunted by the same crimes, right?"

"I don't really know. Seriously. I think I'm just missing in action—an MIA. That can somehow be solved. But I don't know for sure."

What to do now? They had been ignoring their dilemmas. It had been a time to live in a time of death, a blessing whose fragility they had both chosen not to shatter.

Hans opened another bottle of wine. "No matter what happens, it has been a period of great and profound pleasure to me. I've never enjoyed our music so much. I'm sure that pleasure was intensified because it could end at any second. It has, in fact."

"Yes, and I, too, must put a great and bloody puzzle together now. Neither of us can avoid our situation. Of course, you have known the Gastons so much longer than the 'forever' that it seems I have, but Hans, we must figure a way to leave that will save them any more anxiety. They, the château, the farm, the Didots, the herdsmen, and all the local families that depend totally on the Gastons for sustenance, must be saved from us. You and me."

"I am, I think, so selfish, Corporal. I can only think of the welfare and the precious talent of Philippe and Renée."

"Don't feel badly, Hans. It is natural. Along with Eva, you have given the whole world something rare."

"Well . . . I don't. . . ."

Ty interrupted, "No, it is natural, I tell you. We must not regret, we must solve the problem." Suddenly he exclaimed, "I have Lucky Strikes—in my pack—I just remembered them. Hans," he said excitedly, "this is an omen! A sure sign!"

He leapt up and hurried to his knapsack in the other room. He returned with two packs and tossed one to Hans. They opened them as if they were the last caviar on earth and lit them feverishly. Both men inhaled deeply and after exhaling raised the new glasses of wine.

Ty toasted. "May we solve all our troubles by dawn!"

Hans laughed and pushed his bushy hair back. "Yes. Yes, indeed, even though the dawn will be as hidden as a hibernating bear."

They laughed together now while the good thoughts could still come. They knew their situation was ridiculously complicated. They knew they were ridiculous, but this made their shared laughter the exact right medicine.

Soon they went to bed, ready for the unseen dawn.

twenty-three

Hans, exhausted fell asleep immediately. Ty could not sleep. He must connect to one of his grandfather's air-messages. First though, he had more to say to the old man.

"The sandy mist is thinning, Papa J. I'm feeling the actuality now. I use the word feeling because of course, I could never recall every incident even if the bomb hadn't got me. Yes. A bomb. That's what got me. One of our own.

"I was unconscious for a spell, but now I see the puzzle fitting into a bigger picture. All I'll ever have anyway. Yes, with the few remaining mobile members of my squad, we fought to take the lower part of Hill 192, and then turned it over to the 29th Division. We fought on their left flank taking Saint-Lô. Since our bombs had fallen so erratically because of the wind-blown smoke, it was quite a chore.

"As you know from your personal participation in the first-numbered-war-to-end-all-wars, the Germans must never be underestimated as fighters. They rose out of their foxholes behind the fortress hedgerows and it took us somewhere near 20,000 casualties and three days and nights to break a seam in their line. Without that seam, we would have been stuck, maybe knocked back—back to the beaches. You've probably read the rest in the newspaper by now, anyway, and only a dogface infantryman would know the hellacious details. So, you probably know this critical battle better than I do.

"There is no use telling you, who has been there, of all the bone and organs that were abused and scattered on an earth that was itself abused. Hell, Papa J, in those three days at Saint-Lô that seemed like years, we irrigated a lot of Normandy farmland with American blood.

"Now, here's the ace-high-straight-flush, I don't remember anything after those three days until I saw the ground littered with blackbirds from a concussion. I will tell you with great pleasure someday—in person, I hope—the gift of unfiltered magic that I received next. My letter is too long. It is time you wrote to help me solve an even greater puzzle that has an immediacy beyond my thought-words."

Ty relaxed a bit now and soon as if his grandfather was across the room, the mind-letter came.

"First, my son, a little local gossip. True Benson's wife finally got a divorce. She took most of his cash, his cats, his dogs, and the old dun horse he loved so much. She left him half-interest in the stock-farm—as long as he gave her half what it produced. You know that he is the only survivor that served with me in the last great-and-ugly misunderstanding. He was a friend all the way through grade school to college, and the trip to France and Belgium.

"Ty, my son, listen carefully. In your lifetime, you will only have four or five friends who will lie, steal, and protect your back no matter what. I'm speaking here of a long lifetime, Ty. Well, True Benson was one of those. No matter how forcefully I testified that True was a true friend and beacon of heavenly light, it was wasted. A cockeyed little photo, a snapshot did him in. You know the custom in this part of the world about the young boys losing their virginity in a Juárez whorehouse? Of course you do. Your Uncle Josh took you and the Waverly boys for your initiation. Well, True was chosen to deliver his four nephews all at once. He waited, visiting with the landlady—well, manager, if you wish. One of his group snapped a casual picture. He paid no attention. Who would, in a Juárez house of some repute? Well, True's wife, Madge found it and secretly had it blown up close to life-size. Can you believe it? Her lawyer drug it out in the courtroom, and, as they say, the final whistle had blown. It was not only the photo, but the pleasant grin on True's face that said it all. A man happy doing his duty for his nephews, but read differently by the court. They called it licentious and demeaning to all do-gooders. Of course, this is not true because True goes to church every single Sunday. I know because I go with him and your Mama Jo as well. Good God! After the verdict, True told the judge that he had always believed the old saw that a photograph was worth a thousand words but he now knew for an unalloyed fact, that the wrong photograph was worth a million words and possibly that many dollars. Anyway, Ty, a feller must do what he truly feels is right even if it turns out wrong.

"I've often wondered what life is worth. Is one worth more than another? Do you think an old gimpy-legged plug of a horse who never could or would run or pull is worth the same as a Derby winner? It is as mysterious as gravity. You can't breathe very long without being presented with choices. Well, you know that. It is as certain as beans and cornbread. Whether we like it or not we have to decide and get going. Count your blessings or your bruises later, when the duty is done. It's time to feed the chickens. And if you have the time," he chuckles at his own pun, "I promised to tell you a little more about that intangible word. Time has a strong will. It can fly in a circle, backwards as fast as forwards, and in all directions and up and down, at any speed or slowness. It can accelerate so fast that it is invisible even to itself. Everything. Everything is controlled by time, even time itself. Time created thought and the word forever. Time can make a person famous or foolish. To a hummingbird a day is an entire season. A turtle's entire winter hibernation is less than a minute. It's time for you to get going. Time for you to. . . ." Papa J's voice faded away.

Ty lay there enjoying the soothing sound even though the voice was gone. All his muscles, even those in his brain, had relaxed as he listened to his grandfather's wise voice. Part of this was, of course, finishing the picture with all the paint available to him. It was enough. He was no deserter. He was an M.I.A. With this knowledge available to him, he was free to have ideas again. He was deluged with them, cascading in iridescent scenes of prophecy, of hope, of choices.

He leapt from the cot and lit a couple of extra lamps. He wanted light on Hans as he explained the whole world and all that was in it.

"Wake up, Hans. It's solved." He lifted him upright to a sitting position as Hans blinked awake reaching for his spectacles with his hair wild as an old lion's mane.

"Wha . . . what?"

"I've got it. We can save ourselves. You are worth too much to Philippe and Renée, and to millions of people who will hear all three of you. In my opinion, you three are worth more than a million other people. You will give pleasure to the entire world, Hans."

No matter how much Hans protested and puzzled, Ty went right on. "Here's the plan. Simple and clear. Didot can build a false bottom in a horse-drawn wagon that opens from the inside. We will both hide in there, and Didot will drive us close to the front. Then I'll turn you over to the United States Army as a German prisoner of war. Then you'll be safe. You'll be a POW instead of a deserter. When the war ends, as even the most terrible finally do, you will be a free man. You can continue your wonderful career with Philippe and Renée. All three of you will give inspiration and pleasure to the whole world." Ty paused for breath. "Now, how does that sound to you?"

Hans thought a full minute, then said, "But, Ty, you will put your own life in jeopardy."

"No. I'll return to my squad—if I can find any of them alive. Hans, you will be safe as an American POW. Understand? And you can return honorably—or stay here in paradise forever." Ty couldn't believe Hans wasn't instantly overjoyed by his reasoning. "Hey, this is a plan of divine genius. No one will ever know."

"I will."

"Hans, dear Hans, what does it matter? Nothing can happen. I've already been killed and come back to life. I'm immune now. Don't you see?"

Hans was beat. It was going to take more than a moment for this to be absorbed. Finally, the proposition became clear, and Hans became excited.

"My God." He said in German, "There is hope again. It might just work. Yes. It will work." He smiled widely, brushing his mane with both his delicate long-fingered hands. "Yes! Yes!"

Hans made them some coffee, and they sat smoking their Lucky Strikes and planning.

The euphoria was short-lived. There was the unmistakable sound of rolling steel balls. Someone was moving the church pew that concealed the entrance to the underground sanctuary.

Corporal Hale grabbed his rifle and dropped to the floor, aiming down the hallway at the stairs.

The rollers stopped. There was a muttering, and then one pair of feet cautiously felt its way down the stairway, then another. Ty caught a glimpse of a shoe. As she stepped down, Renée's skirt was pulled up, revealing the leg that Ty knew so well and loved so much. He rose and moved into the rock runway. She had made it all the way down now, and those legs sped her toward him. She actually leapt into his arms and yelled, "Ty! My darling Ty!"

She stepped back, examining him. "You're all right. You really are. And Hans?"

Hans stepped out into the passageway, smiling. "Yes, me too. We're all right, together."

She grabbed Ty again, putting her head against his chest to be sure his heart was beating.

It was truly enough to make a grown man cry. So Ty cried, while Hans and Philippe smiled their approval.

twenty-four

It was midmorning of the second day since Ty and Hans had eluded the OSS. They had moved swiftly once Philippe had approved the plan. Didot and one of his sons were working on building the false bottom and escape hatch in the wagon bed. Renée remained noncommittal. Her silence bothered the men, but they could see no other way of doing this. They knew she feared the plan would fail, but they saw this as their only chance. Hans had to be delivered to a group of newly captured German prisoners who were being removed from very near the front lines. They had no idea at all where the front was or would be by the time they found it. Somehow they had to time Hans's arrival perfectly so there would be no chance for the Americans to look too closely at his identification.

The wagon was finished and proudly exhibited by Didot before sunset. The latches and hinges were on the top inside the wagon to make entering and exiting easier. Didot had tested them many times, and not once did they fail. This gave confidence to Hans and Ty. Blankets had been tacked to the bottom of the wagon to ease the discomfort of the jolting ride. Dried meat and apricots were stored under the wagon seat for sustenance along with a jug of water. Although water would be available at farmhouses along the way, they wanted to avoid human contact as much as possible. If stopped by American or German soldiers, or even the French Underground, Didot was to say that he was looking for a buyer for the grain he was carrying in the wagon. This would be plausible, they hoped, since so many farmers had had their supplies taken by the retreating soldiers. Ty marveled at Didot. He and his son had prepared the device with great skill in the face of unknown danger. Didot seemed anxious for the dangerous journey to start early tomorrow, but here he was calmly helping Mme Didot serve the evening meal—and it was a meal for the ages. Philippe's wine-time started the festivities, of course. Then there was squab baked in a lemon sauce so tender that seemed to chew and swallow itself, and potatoes scalloped and seasoned with wild herbs. There was thinly sliced tomatoes in olive oil and a sprinkling of leafy basil. More wine and then a perfect crème brûlée.

They talked of the upcoming journey, of music, and of the world that would soon be free. That world would crave music as people's souls healed. And the evening drew slowly to a close.

Renée had gone into her shell even before that. Suddenly, she emptied her wine glass, bowed deeply, and walked out, saying over and over, "Well, pardon me, pardon me."

The men were noticeably silent for a short spell, then Ty offered the last of his Lucky Strikes and lit them for all three. They enjoyed the last smoke together, but they were painfully conscious of Renée's absence.

Abruptly Philippe stubbed his smoke out and looked directly into Ty's eyes. "She has gone to the pond," he murmured.

Ty took the cue. As he walked in the light of the rising moon, he could hear crickets and night birds talking tunes. A great barn owl swooshed the air away as it dived for a field mouse. Back at the château farmyard, a Didot dog barked back, and one of the dogs from a neighboring rental farm answered, seeming miles away and slightly forlorn. A smaller owl hooted and hooted as the moon rose over the murmur of the little creek.

Ty crossed the bridge where the feathers of a bird had touched his cheek. Reflexively, one hand reached for the spot, and he felt the magical touch as if it had just happened. Then he saw her. His Renée.

She had been swimming along, and now she was out of the pool rubbing her body dry with her hands. There was a double moon now—one in the sky and one mirrored in the long pond. They both reflected Renée's naked skin. Ty's breath came heavier. He ached to rush to her, but knew better than to intrude on her privacy. As she dressed, he hid behind some bushes. He closed his eyes as she walked past. Every particle of whatever made him a man, a man who loved Renée Gaston, was disturbed greatly. He somehow held himself back. He had imposed enough. Now he must face the time of his decision just as his grandfather had mind-written him. It was painful not to run to her. Hold her. Love her. He could hear and feel the music of the mountain floating from her moist body as clearly as he could see the moonlight on her belly.

Now he looked. She was gone somewhere out of his sight. He walked slowly to the bridge and sat on it a long time listening, for what might be the last time, to the little creek that had become the Ganges of his existence.

The night moved slowly. Ty was unable to sleep. That most elusive of all things, time, revealed yet once again the ability to contract like a pair of pliers or become as flexible as a flight of balloons. The night seemed to go on forever.

"Papa J, I must write you this last short letter, for now anyway. I just want to thank you again for all the wonderful reading. And though you knew I was, and still am, a musical dunce, you kept after me until I grew to love music, until it was an element of my

blood. *You were so right to insist that I didn't have to understand the notes and other details to listen and absorb. It was more than decent for you to allow me to attend the little university in Las Vegas, New Mexico. I felt so at home there and in the house of Emilio and Elena Cortez. I know you would have liked for me to attend your alma mater, MIT. Although you never mention that you somehow went from junior college to that great school and became a petroleum engineer, everyone in Lea County knows it. I know it was hard for you to trust me alone in the prairies when I was so small. Thanks for letting me have responsibilities and teaching me so subtly that appreciation for little things is the greatest gift of all. Simple appreciation. You showed me instead of telling me. Thank you."*

He lay back and thought of Renée. At that instant he heard a small knock at the door. Or had he? He rolled toward the door, just barely able to see in the dim light. Renée dropped her nightgown on the floor. She stood silent a moment.

"I must break my vow." She moved astride him and said, in his ear, "It's my fertile time of the month. Now you will have to return."

The moon finished setting as they moved together again and again, sweating with passion. Again, the mystery of time. It was but a brief moment and forever, all at once.

Ty lay back in satiated exhaustion. He knew she was gone, but had not been aware of her leaving. It was better that way; what a wise woman! Or maybe she was trying not to part from him. They were physically separated now, alone in their private rooms, but together in their souls. Always, in all ways.

twenty-five

They were leaving at daybreak.

Mme Didot brought two goosedown pillows, saying, "Renée insisted." Later they would be thankful for this last gesture from the singer. Ty made little prayers that she wouldn't put in an appearance as they departed. She didn't. She couldn't. Neither one could handle another good-bye.

Suddenly Ty raced back into the house and entered the great room. He looked up at Eva's portrait, into eyes the green of Renée's. He said very softly, "She will sing. I promise, Eva." He bowed to the portrait, replaced his helmet, and raced outside.

The two hugged Philippe briefly, strongly. Hans in his military uniform entered the box first. They had decided that the two soldiers would remain hidden inside in the wagon as long as they were in familiar territory. The theory advanced by Philippe that you never really know your neighbors must not be put to the test, not now, when so much was at risk.

Ty crawled in behind Hans and snapped the latches. It was a very dark wooden prison, but the smell of the clean wool blankets helped and at least he was not alone.

Philippe had drawn a map for Didot tracing out the route he thought would be safest. He had pinpointed the fluid-and-staggered war front as well as he could from listening to the radio reports of the underground.

Didot flipped the reins at the two matched gray workhorses. The journey had begun. Philippe stood a moment staring after them. The War Beast creates the strangest actions of all the so-called arts.

In less than a quarter-mile the two soldiers were feeling every crease and pebble in the road and both blessed the women for the blankets and pillows.

Mme Didot went on cleaning the kitchen after the early breakfast. Renée stood in her nightgown on the long balcony and watched the wagon go in and out of sight through the rolling landscape until it disappeared. She was motionless. Then she took a deep breath, pushed back a long strand of her auburn hair, and turned back to the familiar world of Château Gaston. Her desires were so secret that she herself didn't know what she hoped for.

Didot drove through the village waving greetings and encouragement to its survivors. The only public building standing was the church, but people were already rebuilding the other ruins. Wherever there were a few walls steady enough to be built around, there were large cairns of rocks already sorted and stacked according to size. French villages had been rebuilt so often through the centuries that it had simply become ingrained in the survivors to complete the job as soon as possible. Then they could survive for another two or three decades, cultivating the rich land for their families. As fast as the graveyards filled, new villagers were born. As always, the crows cawed their way through history seemingly unaware of its ever-changing course.

When they arrived at the site of General Eubank's defeat, Didot stopped the wagon and allowed Ty to lift the board. Didot held it up so they could see where the Allies had snuffed the breath from the general's entire staff. The eerie brownish/black vehicles had been dragged from the roadway. Someday they would be worth cutting up for parts or shipping to a smelter for recycling into household items, automobile parts or even more war weapons. The earth would finally reclaim its minerals, but it might be hundreds or even thousands of years. If the Beast of War kept on improving the weapons of destruction, inevitably the century would arrive when everything vanished. The Beast had the unrelenting power of gravity. When that day came, the village stones would go unsorted and the crows would no longer caw.

Ty had already seen so much destruction that it bored him, but Hans could not help enjoying the spectacle. The dead men were his countrymen, but they were his enemies nonetheless, having torn him from his music and forced him underground.

Soon they were back in the wagon, once again enduring the dirt and buried rock roads of rural Normandy. Each time Didot would pull up to visit with other travelers or farmers, the sweat came into the palms of their hands, and Ty could not help squeezing his rifle as if in readiness to do battle. It was a jolting, tiring ride, but in Ty's mind it had to be endured so that Hans and Philippe could make music and Renée could sing to it. Before any of it could happen, amidst the biggest human conflict and chaos the world had ever known, the delivery of Hans must be timed perfectly.

At intervals that seemed very far apart, Didot would select a safe spot where they could crawl out and relieve themselves and stretch their cramped muscles.

Didot had a World War I Springfield rifle under the wagon seat along with the dried meat and fruit. He was prepared to do battle or feed his passengers, whatever proved more important. He kept the map inside his shirt and constantly checked it.

They spent the first night in the house of a compatriot, Pierre Sociale. The horses were watered, and then they hid the wagon in a large hay barn. Their hosts fed them well, and even gave them some Calvados to drink after the plain, but plentiful meal of boiled potatoes, garden spinach, and pork. In spite of her hospitality, Mme Sociale looked askance at Hans. She and Pierre had lost both a son and a daughter in the great conflict with Hitler. Hans's musical talent and desertion from the enemy army did little to diminish their hatred for the uniform he wore. This silent hostility seemed to escape Didot, but the two fugitives were aware of it, and deeply uncomfortable. As welcome as a bed would have been, both Hans and Ty were relieved that Pierre so readily agreed when they insisted on sleeping on the hay in the barn. Neither one trusted madame. Her hurt and hatred were too deep. Who could blame her? Her two children were in the ground forever at the hands of the Nazi soldiers.

Hans and Ty took turns watching the house that night. The next night would be one for sleep regardless of how rough the road was.

The following day, just a little after noon, Ty recognized the tentacles of the Beast. Up and down the line, heavy artillery on both sides were firing intermittently, creating a constant growling rumble.

The wagon stopped. He heard German voices. Then one voice took control, commanding Didot to reveal his travel plans. Didot explained that he was delivering seed grain to a cousin some three or four miles distant. The commander of the patrol ordered a soldier to be sure there was only grain in the wagon. In German army fashion, the soldier attached a bayonet to his rifle, leapt onto the wagon, and began jabbing his bayonet between the stacks of grain.

Didot almost gave the game away by reaching for the rifle, but brought up dried apricots instead. He offered them with an unconvincing smile to the commander, who waved them away officiously.

The first thrust of the bayonet penetrated the false bottom exactly between Ty and Hans, touching the real bottom but not sticking. The second thrust plunged into the space between Ty's legs just below his privates. He actually felt the bayonet as it was pulled back up. Both he and Hans braced for steel to enter their bodies, but the next thrust just touched the heel of Hans's boot.

Ty was prone to uncontrollable laughter when faced with a ridiculous statement or action. This was ridiculous. He had always imagined he would be struck by lightning, drowned in a flood, or killed in a car or horse wreck, but here he was, about to exit this earth by way of a Nazi bayonet shoved through sacks of feed. It took the ultimate in self-control but he contained his mirth.

He put his two hands one on top of the other over his midsection for instinctive protection. His muscles tightened and he held his breath, bracing for the bleeding to come. Then he decided to fight rather than gamble on the bayonet missing a fourth time. Ty removed the .45 from the holster and was reaching for the release latch when the German soldier leapt from the wagon and gave the all-clear to his superior. Ty's hand nearly fell apart as he slid the .45 to his side and breathed again.

"Mein Gott," whispered Hans, also taking in some desperately needed air.

The wagon pulled away as Didot said in German, "Go with God." The jolting of the wagon was now welcome, but they had come back into the war. After awhile Ty yelled for Didot to stop. "We can't luck out like that again," he said. "We'll follow you on foot and hide the best we can behind the wagon." Didot didn't want to travel exposed this way, but the corporal was adamant. So they followed Didot. He had been trotting the horses on smoother stretches to gain time, but now he reined them to a walk to make it easier for Ty and Hans to follow.

Ty thought about giving Hans his .45, but he knew it was futile. Philippe was both a fighter and a musician, but Hans was not so versatile. He could not help it. He was born with hands that were made to touch piano keys and copy scores, not pull triggers. The balance of power between these two domains was heavily in favor of triggers. So Ty knew he had to be as alert, as ready, as he had ever been. In this battle of giant armies the enemy could come from any direction or even descend from above.

The two soldiers soon felt the August heat. They were sweating and breathing deeply. Even with all the physical activity at the Gastons,' Ty felt out of shape for battle, but that was soon forgotten as they moved closer to the chaos. The firing came from everywhere and nowhere. He could now actually differentiate the anguished scream of the German 88s and the flatter death whistle of the American 105s and 150s. The 88s always seemed to CRACK and the American artillery had more of a THUMP. The German machine guns and machine pistols fired so fast it was almost one continuous sound, as if the lead blasting at you were all one serpentine bullet. That was why the German weapon was called a burp gun. One lonely loud BURP sent a dozen or more bullets seeking flesh. The cough of the mortars sounded the same from both sides. They cleared their throats almost the same and seemed to be silent a thousandth of a second before exploding and sending hot fragments of steel in a circle of flesh seeking. Rifles, grenades, mines all were looking for soldiers to kill. Such complexity for such a simple purpose as killing a soldier.

Ty could smell the thin mist of blood floating amid the breezes and bullets. It mixed with the smoke of burning tanks, trucks, Jeeps, radios, and disabled guns of every size and bargain. Soon the inevitable pieces of uncollected bodies began to appear. They were just starting to turn black, waiting for overworked meat wagons. It was a chaotic music that the War Beast danced to, a rhythm never to be forgotten—not even in dreams.

Ty could hardly believe it, but he felt at home now, with the battle and with his fear. He must soon order Didot back to the château and do his duty by Hans and then by himself and his squad.

Then he saw it: the movement of an unmistakably German steel helmet behind a rock-and-tree-lined fence. "Didot!" he called, "Stop. Stop, get down and check your wagon wheels." Didot had fought in the last great war, and all training had returned for this occasion. He felt, smelled, sensed the war the same as Ty. He casually reined the horses to a stop and slowly crawled down to follow Ty's orders.

Ty knelt behind the wagon, motioning Hans to do the same. As Didot carefully checked the wheel next to them, Ty extracted the grenade from his pocket and spoke very softly, firmly, "Now listen carefully. There is an irrigation ditch on the right side of the road. It's a long throw, but I'm going to try the grenade anyway. Even if I don't clear the fence with it, dive for the ditch the second you hear it go off. I'm going to take him—or them. You got it?"

Both Didot and Hans grunted in the affirmative. Ty had killed many rabbits and missed more hurling rocks when the .22 ammunition of his youth was exhausted. He had played baseball, softball, football, and plain catch the whole of his youth. Still, this distance would surely test him. He took a deep breath, pulled the pin, leaned back with the grenade as far as he could and hurled it. His two companions waited for the explosion.

Ty counted, "One. Two. Three," then charged the fence.

He had fortunately timed it exactly right. The grenade explosion dimmed the sound of the large noise makers farther on. He raced low at the fence, the M1 ready as always before. Dust filled the air behind the fence as he closed on it. The secret was to get there before any of the surviving enemy had a chance to overcome the shock.

One sergeant had been blown up and lay on his back across the fence. One arm dangled without a hand. The tendons looked like the threads of a worn-out toy. One eyeball dangled twisting back and forth on his forehead like a large grape on a string.

Ty leapt up on the fence belly-first. He saw two more dead bodies and a third that moved. He shot it still. One had fallen over the fence where it paralleled the road. Before he could make ready, another German soldier, the last in the corner still alive, raised up right under Ty and stabbed upward with his bayonet. It caught in the sleeve of Ty's right arm. Ty pulled the bayonet from the dazed soldier's hand and jabbed with all his adrenaline strength. The blade went between the eyes, passing through the lower brain, and shoved bone aside as it exited the back of the man's head.

All was not done here. Ty fell back and hit the ground rolling as he got his rifle under control. A huge German private staggered around the corner with a burp gun. He whirled to eradicate Ty, but a bullet from the Didot's World War I rifle entered one temple with a dark round hole and exited the other, tearing a jagged exit three times as big as the entrance wound. The soldier fell heavily, some ancient instinct causing him to discharge the burp gun twice into the earth as he fell to the final position.

Ty sat up. He raised his clasped hands above his head in a grateful salute to Didot, who sat holding the stomping horses with one hand on the reins and the old rifle above his head in the other.

Ty scrambled to his feet, rolled to the corner of the fence, found his rifle, and moved to the front of the wagon to be sure the roadway was clear and safe. It was for now. The little battle was over right here, but was being repeated in thousands of distant places that very instant.

Ty walked over to Didot, laughing, "You old goat, you disobeyed orders."

"No, I didn't," he laughed back, "I outranked you. I was a Sergeant Major."

Even Hans joined the mirth. They had won. Their own blood was in the victory surge. Ty's spontaneous laughter that often embarrassed even him could escape harmlessly now, and he laughed until he fell to his knees. After he had laughed away the tension, Ty became deadly serious. He checked his rifle and the .45.

Didot was having trouble with the horses. They wanted to bolt. The firing of the guns and the smell of fresh human blood had stirred up ancient memories of battle. Ty eased over beside them as they stomped the ground, chomped their bits, and pulled against the reins held taut by Didot. Ty remembered the best horse trainer in Lea County on the CX ranch. Slim Harris talked slowly and softly to the horse, then touched it gently before slipping a hackamore over its nose and head.

Ty was purring. "You *are* great horses. You are from a line of famous warriors who fought the Vikings. Easy always does it. Just calm it down. Easy. Easy now. Ah, that's it, fine horse. Fine gentlemen, you are. Now, let Didot turn you around and late tomorrow you will be in your cozy stall at the Gaston farm eating oats and hay. That's it. Good horse. Good horses." Horses may not understand the meaning of calming words, but they sure recognize the feeling. The horses settled down as Ty patted and rubbed each in turn along the neck.

Didot reined the horses expertly around. They were calm now. But soon they would pick up their gait no matter what Didot wanted. Horses have a home-compass in their heads somewhere. They always know. Always.

Didot climbed down, rubbed at his mustache, and hugged Hans. Then he turned to Ty and almost crushed the breath from him. Tears were in his eyes.

Ty choked his tears back, saying in French, "Thanks for saving my life, Didot."

"You saved mine first, Sir."

"Nothing. My job. Please give our love to the Gastons and tell them we're safe because of your driving and accurate shooting."

Hans had a hard time speaking but finally choked out, "Yes, give them our love. And I'll see them soon, someday.... We'll see them soon. Our love." He could say no more. Hans stood like a tree, watching Didot letting the team of grays take him home to Château Gaston.

Ty moved and took Hans's arm, "Come. Our duty is with you now. They will need you...." The rest went unsaid.

They were following a fence line studded with poplar trees. A roadway was on the other side. A very busy roadway. Trucks loaded with ammo and other supplies were headed for a makeshift quartermaster depot. They were the famed Red Ball Express, mostly driven by black American soldiers, which never stopped moving.

Hans and Ty soon grew accustomed to the sounds and smells. It was much easier for Ty. He had spent weeks that seemed like years in the middle of it all earlier on.

The grinding of the hedge-busting tanks dominated all. They could hear, smell, and only occasionally see long staggered lines of steel and flesh moving forward towards Berlin and even Czechoslovakia. The two had to be ready to dive into the irrigation ditch any second.

The ditch ran out at the edge of a large town. The outlying houses had been shelled or bombed out. Heaps of furniture, clothing, curtains, pots, and pans were everywhere. The people had gone. They were hiding in the timbered hills, in the homes of farmers whose houses had escaped the bombs, hiding anywhere they thought they could keep their young children from the two life-grinding forces.

Ty and Hans walked into town, from house to house, yard to yard. Most were hollow shells. Some stood miraculously in the middle of the rubble, empty, grinning ghosts, but standing nevertheless.

Everywhere they smelled the scent of war and saw bloody clothing scattered in little piles where it had been cut from the wounded. The dead civilians as well as soldiers were removed with their garments intact. Even the standing buildings were marked by bullets and shrapnel fragments. Nothing had escaped the frenzy of the street fighting, but the battle was over. The enemy had retreated.

Ty kept Hans behind him, signaling to him with hand movements as they slowly, cautiously, inched their way through the town. They could hear the sounds of battles south of town, but they could ignore it for now. Somewhere to their right, a main highway was open, and they could hear the drone of thousands of supply vehicles. They dodged, crawled, raced from corner to corner, hugging any buildings that didn't seem likely to fall on them. They covered about one block per hour.

Every now and then they found a soldier's body the medics or the meat wagons had missed. Splashes of red were everywhere, along with the debris of the wounded: helmets, guns, packs, and now and then a photo of a loved one, a cigarette lighter, or a comb. Some were German items, some were American. The enemy had fought for every door, floor, and window in this town. All had paid a very high price indeed.

The surviving people of the town would return and finally, laboriously repair it. The shredded and broken bushes and trees would grow back, but the German and American soldiers who had murdered each other here would never return. Never.

Then Ty had a feeling. Someone was across the street. He motioned Hans to stop. He crawled to the corner and peered out looking both ways, rifle ready. Ty put the German soldier in his sights just as he bolted out the door. There were two of them. He pulled the trigger and the bullet told him he had made a kill. The soldier buckled at the knees as the bullet struck his heart knocking a rib in half as it exited. His upper body whipped back, and he fell facing Ty his rifle thrown several feet ahead.

The second soldier was a step behind him. He whirled back towards the doorway. Ty fired the second time a fraction of a second too late. The German soldier had made it back inside. Ty had seen the flash of the scope on the rifle. A sniper. They never gave up. That was Hitler's training, the brainwashing of children, and it worked. He had experienced how well it worked too many times already.

Ty was pissed at himself. He had shot the wrong man. He should have shot the sniper.

He jumped up, motioning Hans to follow him into the building. The stairways were solid even though someone had thrown a grenade into the second story. Ty felt regret again. He had failed to secure another grenade from one of the many dead in the town, an oversight that could doom their mission. His absolute duty was to deliver Hans as a POW so he could survive to make music for the world, especially for Renée. It was all absolute.

On the second floor, they took a room next to the street directly across from the three-story building containing the sniper. He had them under his control. The adjoining building was demolished. The sniper had a field of fire on them from the third-floor corner window. The structure they occupied had once been an apartment building. The grenade had torn boards loose, and they lay scattered about the room amid broken pieces of stucco. A bed was blown away from the wall. Hans chose to huddle there.

Ty went to work. He set his helmet above the window sill on one of the shattered boards. Nothing. The sniper was a real pro. How did he know the helmet was a decoy? Staying below the window and behind the brick of its walls, Ty tried raising the helmet from several spots. Nothing. He sat on the floor and pondered a moment.

"All right. Stay prone where you are, Hans. I'm going to try something else." He moved to a corner. Then, at full speed, he ran past the open double window. Nothing. Then again. Nothing. Silence except for their breathing.

Once more the bullet caught the back of his combat shirt and knocked a chunk of loose plaster from the far wall. The sniper had outwitted him, missing the swift moving target by a fraction of a second.

"Well, the bastard outsmarted me, but now we know he is never going to quit."

Hans spoke with surprising calm. "What do we do?"

"Wait. We have to outwait him. Make him come to us. He'll have to win this. In his mind, he is a traitor to Hitler if he lets us get away."

"I can wait," Hans said.

Ty lay down against the wall and rested his rifle across his belly. He took the .45 out of the holster and placed it by his side. Hans pulled a ripped blanket from the bed and stretched out against the opposite wall. They hadn't realized how tired they were. When there are a few moments of stillness in war, the weariness comes irresistibly.

The door where Hans rested had been blown apart. There was one long, sharp-pointed board close by. He picked it up fearfully and placed it by his side where he lay on the shrapnel-ripped blanket. For the first time in his musical life he craved a weapon. He knew Ty would never let him have a firearm, so this would have to do. The truth, of course, was that the caveman weapon made him feel even more vulnerable.

Across the street Helmut Burger was feeling a slow rage turn more and more heated. He had been groomed to be a sniper. At the age of nine, he outshot everyone in the Hitler youth class no matter what their age. That meant he was a superior to several hundred highly trained and indoctrinated children. Burger had certainly lived up to his promise. The soldier across the street had been teasing him. A mistake. He had notched thirty-nine kills and wanted desperately to make his military record read at least an even forty. He had been insulted by the helmet on a stick, teased as if he were an amateur. That was one of the first things he learned in sniper school: the different look a helmet had with a real live head in it. Now he had missed a fast-moving target. A telescope was not made for that. When it got dark he would exit the rear of his building and slowly, carefully make his way to the lair of his antagonist. Even if it took all night, he would climb the stairs and kill him with a shot exactly between the eyes. He wanted to see the life fade away. That was what all the years of training had been for. That was what the regimentation of nerves and the practice firing of thousands of rounds had been for. Yet, he had never got to witness this close-up. All thirty-nine shots had been from thirty yards or more. He was always too late to observe death taking the light from the eyes. Now he would get it all.

The moon was half full and his 20/20 eyes would adjust like a cat's. He checked the bolt action that most German snipers used, an American Springfield rifle from World War I. It was his favored weapon. Oh, what pleasure awaited. This man was doomed to die by his own gun, in a sense. Poetic justice comes to all who seek as strongly, as resolutely as he, Sergeant Major Helmut Burger of the 2nd SS Battalion, one of Herr Hitler's favorites.

The gun was ready. Burger was always ready. He moved out to do what he was born to do. Kill.

twenty-six

Ty went into a half/vision in spite of the danger across the
street. He had to receive at least one more mind-letter
from his grandfather, since the morning would bring about
the sniper's demise or his. If he made it, Hans must be saved and
become an American POW, so his vow to Eva and their wishes for
Renée could come true. So he started to talk to his grandfather.

"Ah, Papa J, I've experienced a little bit of the hand-to-hand busi-
ness that you did in the last one. And hey, I don't much like it. But I
suppose it's no worse than a mortar barrage. I got a look at the Red
Ball Express; that's our biggest trucking supply source here. It's sort of a
back-home-kind-of-thinking process. And I was wondering how much
gasoline from the oil production back in Lea County they have to pump
to help win this cockeyed war. Let's get on with what we've both got to
tell in our mind-letters."

Helmut Burger, super sniper, had made it across the street and was
slowly inching along to the back of Ty and Hans's building. He had
learned to take the time to let his eyes adjust to night vision long
ago. He would look into the moon shadows until he could dis-
cern objects. It was a matter of pure patience. He had a surplus of
patience because he loved the sudden and instant kill that it made
possible. This was a new adventure for him.

Ty could feel Papa J's letter coming.

"*You know, son, how our part of the world comes and goes financially by need and price of oil? Oh, sure, farming and ranching are a basis of our economy, but it's the oil patches that make the wheels turn. The great Permian Basin covers all of southeastern New Mexico and a large part of West Texas. That's big, son. Very big, indeed. That oil is saving the world, whether anyone can admit it or not. There just wouldn't be enough tanks, Jeeps, supply trucks, aircraft carriers, warships of all kinds doing their work, not to mention the thousands of bombers and fighters that never stop, without the production from the Permian Basin. Believe me, the old saw about flipping a coin to see if we all spoke German or Japanese would already have come true. We're doing fine here because we raise so much of our own food. Town folks are another matter. Everything is rationed out by stamps: food, gas, tires, sugar, just about everything. I haven't heard a single bellyacher yet. It's a great country, son. Hell, I'm even running a pump line for Shell Oil to help out a little, I hope. I got the job handed to me because all the young men and women are either gone to fight or build the guns that make it possible. The woman's world has changed forever and for the better. You'll see right off when you get back. They are scattered out all over the land building tanks, uniforms, guns, everything. You'll see the wonderful results when you get back. The doors have finally opened for our women.*"

Burger took his time at the ground floor blown-out door. He tried to imagine himself into moving like the hands of a clock. At last he could see the stairway that would lead him to a new thrill. Maybe his greatest. No maybe about it. No hoping. It would be as he planned and desired. When the Fuhrer read this account of his deed it would be like a Shakespearean drama. He already had the Iron Cross. Maybe he would be assigned to head up the instruction of snipers worldwide. They were going to be in even greater demand to carry out the thousand-year concept. He wanted to be a big part of it. Right now he would inch up the stairs so slowly, so stealthily there would be no warning sound. He actually licked his lips anticipating the instant surprise that would appear on his victim's face. But it was the following instant blankness that he would savor most. He didn't believe in a God, except Hitler, but he knew he was about to be blessed somehow.

"Ty, your grandmother spends half her time gathering scrap metal, tinfoil from wrappers, any material that can be used in making weapons. It doesn't matter what age they are, folks from three to ninety are pitching in and working for the inevitable victory. We want you boys to return home to freedom. There ain't nothing without freedom. Nothing at all for a real human or a deer, a moose, a mouse, a crow, a college student like you and even an old worn-out do-it-all like me. I'll be seeing you before you know it. Fight well, and keep breathing."

Burger was almost up the steps now. There had been one little creak, but it went unheeded, he was sure. Still, it had to be perfect. He was gloating already.

"Well, Papa J, I want to thank you again for all the knowledge and pleasure of fine books and music and life in general that you directed this reluctant child to. Without them I could never have enjoyed and actually savored these last few accidental days to the ultimate as I did. I have no way of expressing, even to you, how infinitely precious and fulfilling they were. Thanks again and mixing it up in proper measure I can only say. Viva le grande intermezzo. Soon. Very soon."

Now Burger was at the top of the stairway, the bolt-action slung over his back. He stood up and took it in his hands where it felt warm, comfortable, alive. He didn't raise a foot, he simply slid one at a time, barely touching the floor.

He stopped at the edge of the doorway to peer into the battered room. The blown-out windows pulled the half moon rays in and lighted the shadows. He could see the sleeping soldier prone on the floor half under the window. Good, he slept with his eyes half open. It would be better than he had dreamed. With the same silent technique he entered the room, finally stopping in the middle of the floor. Even the man of perfect control could feel his chest heave in anticipation of the glorious killing to come. He raised the rifle ever so slowly. He didn't even want to disturb the air itself. The moonlight made things clear to him.

Now he was within inches of his target. He would call out. And as the head tilted towards him, his forefinger would expertly pull the hair trigger to place the bullet exactly between the eyes. And then, the most exciting thrill on earth, witnessing the life disappearing into the void by his own hand.

Ty's half-vision was broken. Something had altered the light in the room. He turned his head and eyes. "Aw, sh . . ."

Something exited the mouth of the man standing there. It was sharp and jagged as revealed by the half moonlight. It was the sharp end of a broken board. Even in the night light, Ty saw the expression of terrible disappointment flash across the face. The countenance of a killer was gone, unseen by anyone. Burger buckled over, firing his gun into the floor about six inches from Ty. Hans jerked the bloody board free. Holding it in both hands, he began stabbing the dead body in the groin, in the stomach, and down into the fixed eyes, inches deep.

Ty yelled with all his strength, "Hans! Hans! Stop. It's finished."

Hans stopped, still staring at the bloody pointed board. Then he opened both hands at once holding them in the air in front of his face. He stared at them. Immobile. The only movement was in his eyes. Then he fell to his knees and sobbed, his entire body jerking.

Ty looked at the scope on the dead man's rifle and said to Hans, "My God, you got the sniper. It's all right, Hans. Everyone in the world wants a sniper. You got yourself one." He pulled Hans to his feet. "Okay, now. We've got to get going. It's almost daylight. Today you'll be a POW. Think of it, Hans, you'll be a free man before long."

For two days they had walked stealthily through the bruised city and were now on the outskirts, moving slowly, alertly down a fencerow. The rock fences with parallel irrigation ditches were convenient places to fall into and hide.

Suddenly they were out of the town and at the edge of their first farm. The property was unharmed, as was the next one. Though the Germans had fought ferociously for the city, they had clearly pulled back to regroup.

Suddenly they faced the first small cluster of returning refugees. It was too late to hide. Ty shoved the rifle in Hans's back. "Keep your hands up," he said in a loud voice. Then, lowering his voice to a whisper, he said, "Act sheepish."

"I am sheepish."

As they passed the refugees, before Ty could say hello and good luck in French, one old woman moved unexpectedly toward Hans and spat in his face.

"Boche, Boche," she growled and tried to spit again but it was only air.

One of the children, around six years old, picked up a rock from the road and hurled it at Hans. Instead, it missed him and hit Ty on the shoulder. He wanted to scold the child, but instantly realized what all was in the poor child's mind: lost loved ones, probably a father, probably displaced from a crumbled house that had been his only home. And all of them in this short line, and the thousands more to come, would soon be digging in the ruins of their lives. There were rotting bodies—their kin, their neighbors—yet to be discovered in the rubble of countless piles of homes. He decided he could take a rock on the shoulder for the child.

The line of refugees passed on. Hans and Ty worked their way sideways seeking the main transportation route where they thought they could find a group of captured Germans being moved to the rear. The battle noise intensified. On a secondary road they now encountered several hundred returning refugees. Some had wagons piled high with household goods: dogs, cats, children, the old and weak, the sick. Ty noticed there were very few eighteen to forty year olds among them. The war had long ago swallowed them.

Ty was overwhelmed, but only for a moment. His mission was to save the life of the man who just saved him from a sniper. He forgot that he had once saved Hans on the way to the underground chambers. If they had been buddies in the same squad, things might be different. But Hans was more than a buddy, or even a child. Hans had to be saved for Philippe and Renée. And on top of that, Ty himself was nowhere near being in the clear unless he rejoined his old outfit before he was found to be missing.

At last there was a gap in the refugee line wide enough so they could move along toward the grinding and roaring of the huge arterial truck line and the heart of the battle, now only two or three miles distant. Ty was thankful they had breached the gap between the returning French refugees and the front. These people had lost their freedom, many lives, and a lot of their dignity because of the Nazi Occupation. He feared that the sight of Hans, a German prisoner with only one lone guard, could inspire a Frenchman to tear Hans to shreds, and himself, as well, if he tried to protect the POW. From now on, the ground would be occupied mostly by heavily armed American soldiers wanting to kill Nazis.

At last, with every ducking and dodging trick they had ever learned, they arrived at a thick clump of evergreen trees next to the main highway. They were mesmerized at the two-way traffic. Trucks full of assorted ammo and trucks with tanks and tank killers, 105s and 150s, mortars and mortar ammunition. There were endless boxes of rifle and machine-gun ammo along with grenades and grenade launchers, and above all gasoline, and food. The energy that made the men and machines work was on the move. Breaking things and killing the enemy was all that was on the menu now.

Returning also were ambulances and Jeeps jerry-rigged as ambulances. There were also the walking wounded, empty supply trucks, command Jeeps, and endless broken machinery waiting to be repaired to fight again.

Then it happened. Three open trucks carrying prisoners moved towards them. Now was the moment. There was no more time to ponder or worry.

Ty jabbed the rifle in Hans's side as he would have done with any prisoner and said harshly, "Move!"

Ty and Hans stepped right out in front of the first POW truck. The driver had to brake or kill them. He stopped about four inches from Hans. The other trucks, jammed close together, were also forced to a stop. Horns were blaring, and curses could be heard.

Ty shouted, as he pushed Hans around to the side of the truck, "Hey, men, make room for another one! Sardine him in there. Hurry. Hurry it up."

"Okay. Okay."

A guard leaned down and grabbed Hans under the arms while Ty shoved at his butt. Hans tumbled over and was finally sandwiched between a captain and a private in the dirty gray uniforms of the shrinking German army.

Ty stood still, leaning on his rifle, staring after the truck. For just a moment he was numb from the special delivery. It was done. Hans was back home at last, until the war was over. He hoped that Hans drew an entertainment-loving commandant who appreciated his music so he could finish out the war playing for everyone in his compound and keep up his skills.

Finally, all the trucks ground into gear and moved away. Without looking back, Ty started down the road towards the front.

Corporal Ty Hale thought of Hans no more. He had to concentrate on looking for someone from his own outfit. He inspected every Jeep rigged for a four-stretcher ambulance that came his way. He ran beside them searching for someone with his insignia.

At last he spotted one. He hadn't been so thrilled since he lost his virginity in a Juárez brothel. There on the soldier's shoulder was the patch of Ty's outfit. Unconscious on a stretcher between two medics, he was suffering from a belly wound. Ty ran beside them trying to yell the injured man awake. Nothing.

He moved to the side of the road and stood a minute looking south toward Paris and Berlin. He decided to go to Berlin. Now he let his truest of natures take over. He was running and running and running. After a while the vehicles thinned until there were mostly one-way ambulances. The 88s and mortars were falling and slamming into the pasture next to him. The newly dead were numerous along the way now. Mostly Americans. Many from his own outfit. He was tempted to seek a familiar face among the dead, but his need to rejoin his squad won out.

The 88s were zipping. The 21-pound shell was crashing into the earth at the speed of 2,690 feet per second. He was running at about 10 feet per second towards them. One of the 88s was very close; a piece of shrapnel broke the stock of his rifle and knocked it from his hand. It didn't bother the corporal at all as long as he could run on. There were plenty of unused guns lying all about the front.

His parents' faces flashed by him, then Jiggs and Mama Jo, and blue-eyed Emilio and Elena whizzed past, along with the members of his squad before the invasion. Philippe, Didot, Hans, and then his own image. All were smiling. Renée, Renée, Renée! She laughed melodically aloud. He could hear it. He could feel it. But he laughed on as well. He ran south. He looked for crows, but they were all cleaning up the messes he had just left behind. He wished he could run all the way to Berlin and kill Hitler. That would be the greatest of missions. He would do it for Hitler's great injury to Eva Gaston, for the hidden part of the bloodlines of Emilio and Elena Cortez.

He laughed louder and louder and ran faster and faster. All the way to hell with Hitler and to hell with the Beast that spawned him. This running, this laughter, these thoughts were his music. He would give it all the basic rhythm he had. There would always be warped brains like Hitler's for the Beast to infuse and infect, but it would be especially nice to help all the millions of soldiers and civilians craving to get off that first shot at the Fuhrer.

The 88s were coming faster and faster. He had never felt so free. He was running faster than he ever had imagined. He felt as if he could turn around and outrace the German artillery, but of course, he could not do that, not now. He must rejoin his squad. He felt as if he was speeding so fast that his feet were only touching the ground every fifth stride. Now every tenth. He was racing towards the land of Wagner.

In a flash of blue light, Corporal Ty Hale was up in the domain of crows. He was sure he floated in air as they did when the wind currents were just right. He looked hard for his cawing brothers and sisters, but before he could locate them, the entire earth of Normandy moved up to greet and meet him.

He could hear all the stones, pebbles, and every grain of sand singing and making music. Surprisingly he understood all the words, notes and movements, and then he heard someone calling, "Medic! Medic!"

It was himself. "Oh, God, oh, please, dear God! Not now! Mama Jo . . . Mama Jo . . . Mama. . . ."

Philippe Gaston and Hans Heinike were playing for Renée in the great Sorbonne Auditorium in Paris. She was finishing an old love song, controlling the audience with her expressive hands as surely as she melted their hearts with her voice. The last note hung in the air like the scent of a thousand acres of roses.

A young man with a slight limp and an angular scar across his forehead that disappeared into his hair left the audience with a sleeping child across his shoulder. He was talking the child gently awake.

The audience was breathless, motionless. Then in one movement they stood applauding wildly through three curtain calls. She made the palms-up motion for the audience to applaud the musicians, Philippe and Hans.

"At last," Renée thought, "I can see my treasures, my husband and my son."

Philippe and Hans followed her through the backstage curtains, where she was greeted by three-and-a-half-year-old Philippe Jiggs Gaston Hale. He broke away from his father's arms and ran to Renée where she squatted waiting and smiling with effervescent joy. The youngster ran like a grownup, his arms pumping like an Olympic sprinter. Laughing wildly, he was swept up in his mother's strong arms. She kissed him over and over and over, while his laughter bounced gaily over everyone. Everywhere.